Praise for *For Sizakele*

For Sizakele is a poetic and intimate journey through the dense thicket of the lives of lovers. Cultural displacement, deep wounds and youthful passion are the backdrop for this vivid series of encounters between women—butch and femme—who must learn to know and trust themselves for love to be possible. Etaghene has created a heartbreaking yet encouraging glimpse at the mountains women of color must climb to see the sunrise.

—Jewelle Gomez, author, *The Gilda Stories*

As African lesbians from South Africa and beyond, especially in places where prejudice, "curative rapes" and brutal murders of us occur in our formative spaces—including our homes, workplaces, churches, schools—we are thirsty for text like *[For Sizakele]*. Our ... communities still lack narratives produced by our own in a manner that we are able to articulate our issues as we choose. *[For Sizakele]* will help our queers, lesbians, dykes, femmes and trans people and encourage each and every one of us to read, write and be read... not forgetting many who can't dare to come out due to sexual orientation and gender expression still outlawed in many countries in Africa and around the globe. It is through this writing that many queer generations after us will get an opportunity to reference what she captured.

—Zanele Muholi, visual activist, author, *Faces and Phases*

FOR *Sizakele*

FOR *Sizakele*

YVONNE FLY ONAKEME ETAGHENE

RedBone Press | Washington, DC

For Sizakele

Published by:
RedBone Press
P O Box 15571
Washington, DC 20003

10 9 8 7 6 5 4 3 2 1

Cover photos © Yvonne Onakeme Etaghene
Cover design: Eunice Corbin
Printed in the United States of America

ISBN 978-0-9899405-1-1 $15.00

For my beloved mother,
Jackelene Nicholas Braie

for every immigrant dyke of color,
dyke of color,
queer person who ever walked into a library
or bookstore
hungry
for a story about their love,
and walked out with an empty stomach:
this is for you

Inside of Me

freedom poem

I want to write a freedom poem

I poured the words into the microphone in front of me, hands outstretched, palms facing downward, riding the air.

a heat rising in my chest
spirit bigger than circumstance
phoenix resurrection
immaculate conversation
conceiving of freedoms sweeter than sunrise

poem.

An audience member in the dimly lit café clapped, murmuring, *"Yes, yes."*

I want to write a poem vigorous
a poem fierce
a poem sharp,
words that slaughter injustice
truth throbbing in my chest,
I want to write a freedom song that dances off my tongue,
vibrating in your soul, to the beat of wind
blowing across desert sands on the distant lands
we hail from
and summon
each time we dance
smile
scream;
I want to write the poem that *is* the dream

we thought we forgot to remember
the December poem in the summer
the heat of August in the winter.

I delicately tilted the microphone closer to my face and slowly breathed in.

I want to write a poem so scary
oil companies won't come near me,
Nigerian river goddess taking back lands from conglomerates
that stole our essence—we taking our natural resources back
and charging a fee,
we won't call it *reparations*
we'll call it
a business transaction,
don't call this
a violent, insurgent rebel faction
call me *the truth*
something *you* ain't used to.
how about land mines confined
to the inner sanctum of your mind
tearing limbs from sockets
behind your eye sockets
is this driving you crazy?
the earth is *not* quaking,
that's *you* shaking.
colonizer:
you fucked with the wrong priestess.
I wrote this in blood last night
so I wouldn't forget,
my tongue etched my truth into my skin,
your sins follow you till they carve your name in tombstone:
R.I.P.:
Resistance

Instigated
Peace.

Audience members clapped enthusiastically, and I smiled.

this poem is
unabashedly, passionately
dedicated to *me*
to my grandmothers, my sisters
my mother, my aunties
to peoples indigenous to where they lay
to Nigeria
to those in exile
to folks who ain't been home in a long, long while
because amerikkkan-funded governments support genocide.
this poem is dedicated to the unnamed
unfamous freedom fighters
to prostitutes and bus drivers
to the unemployed
underpaid
uninsured,
to those in search of cures to kkk-manufactured diseases:
I send this poem to us
on breezes
to keep us cool on the hottest of days
in the belly
of the beast.

I opened my eyes slowly, tenderness in my gaze. The light in the small, intimate café was dark as amber stained glass. I looked beyond the stage into the crowd of young, mostly Black college students sitting in wooden straight-backed chairs, worn couches and armchairs. An espresso machine squealed in the background as if fighting for its life.

The applause that followed my performance was passionate and powerful. As I walked off stage, Xio returned to the mic and said, "Show Taylor some love for that beautiful piece!" The applause deepened as I wove my way through the audience, found my baby and sat down. Lee turned her head to mine, softly bit the edge of my ear, then sucked it with soft lips that sent shivers through me.

"You were *amazing,*" she whispered.

I gave her a quick kiss then pulled away slightly, barely a millimeter between our lips.

"I love you," I said. I relaxed into the crook of her arm. The solid warmth of her body reminded me of how much our love was home to me. I could smell subtle hints of her musky cologne as I snuggled into her.

After the show, we said our goodbyes, hugged our peoples and got into Lee's SUV to drive to her apartment. Lee carefully navigated Lower Manhattan streets, lightly dusted with snow soft as powdered sugar. As we cruised across the Brooklyn Bridge, I was happy we were *finally* alone so I could openly stare at her with wonder and love. Lee's muscular, 5'11" frame sat comfortably in the driver's seat, her Caesar haircut fresh as she leaned back against the headrest. My eyes caught her broad hands grasping the steering wheel: light caramel brown with neatly cut fingernails. My stomach did involuntary flip-flops as I remembered what those fingers felt like inside me. I smiled, licked my lips, and looked away. I felt myself getting wet at just the *thought* of her fingers. Gently thrusting inside me. My legs spread. My ass and back pressed against the bathroom door. Lee on her knees in front of me—

"What you smiling about?"

I cleared my throat unnecessarily. "Nothing," I lied.

"Nothing?" she teased, looking over at me. "Then why you lookin like the dyke who just got her pussy ate?"

I laughed. She read me so easily.

"Because I'm about to be," I said.

"Really? By who?"

"Please." I laughed at the familiar game we played. My left hand glided between her legs and slowly slid up her thigh. "By you, King."

"Sorry baby … my tongue's a little tired tonight." Lee's voice was all low and shit—fucking with me like she *knew* I liked to be fucked with.

"Whateva. Do some exercises and get ready for me."

ꕥ

Lee stopped before she opened her apartment door.

"Wait out here," she said.

"What? Why?"

"Trust me."

She went inside while I waited and wondered what could possibly be going on in there. A few minutes later, she returned.

"Close your eyes," she said.

"Wha—"

"Taylor. Just trust me."

I closed my eyes and she carefully led me into the apartment.

I took a few tentative steps as she guided me; then she said, "You can open your eyes now."

I saw a sea of golden flames. Candles on top of every surface—the coffee table, the windowsills, the floor, the small table by the door where we dropped our keys.

"Lee …"

"Come with me."

I followed her to the bedroom. Candles on the dresser, nightstand and floor set the dark room aglow. The walls were alive with the shadows of the flames. "What's all this?" I asked, captivated.

"A year ago today, we went on our first date together," Lee said.

I turned around and looked up into her eyes.

Lee smiled. "Happy anniversary, baby."

"My King! I didn't even know we were celebrating!"

"Surprise!" She said it with such sweetness, I ached looking at her. I kissed her, smiling. I couldn't believe she was so fuckin thoughtful.

My hands, vibrating with desire, peeled and pulled off Lee's clothes. I pressed my skin, the color of soil after rain, lovingly into Lee's body. We tumbled onto the bed—thirsty hands drinking, hungry hands devouring.

Straddling her sides, I grabbed the top of her shoulders and rode her with my strap-on, pushing myself deeper into her pussy. My grinding elicited groans from her lips that sent shivers rushing over my clit. Moonlight streamed through the window blinds, making designs across her breasts. The tips of my fingers teased the tips of her nipples. She groaned, reached up and sunk her fingers into my twists. I loved how her hands wrapped around my hair, pulling on it harder and harder as her pleasure rose.

"Tayl …" she started.

"Uh-huh, baby," I said with a smile.

"Ouuu …" she moaned.

Smiling, I whispered, *"I know, baby."*

Lee grabbed my hips, pulling me deeper into her. Her hands rushed up to my bare breasts as she urgently increased the speed of our grinding. My eyes sought hers. Lee's moans came and rose in echoes, higher and wider and deeper. Making love to Lee was an extended climax: each touch made me shiver and shake, giving me goose bumps. I loved watching ecstasy flood her face. Her eyes drifted closed, her breathing deepened and her groans grew louder and louder until they just … stopped. Her hands gripped my hips tightly and the sweetest gasp escaped her lips as I shivered above her and she shook beneath me—our sweat and wetness humming and buzzing…

I love making love to Lee.

FOR SIZAKELE

ૡ

Waking up in Lee's arms, cuddled into her warm nakedness, was luscious perfection. I remembered last night and smiled, nuzzling closer to her. The only light around us was dawn birthing herself, her rays gradually meandering onto the walls, the sheets and our skin, protecting us from the harsh January winter. In a sleepy haze, I tenderly wrapped my lips around Lee's breast, gently sucking on her nipple. My tongue made relaxed, sensual patterns like she was velvet I could leave an imprint of my love on. The alarm went off, making my heart jump. Slightly aggravated, I rolled my eyes and hit the off button. I reluctantly slipped out from under the thick comforter away from my lover, squinting to find my panties, the peace of five seconds ago lost.

"Where you goin?" Lee mumbled sleepily.

"Back to my room to shower and change for class," I said, wiggling into my pants.

"Skip."

"Can't" I said, smiling. "I gotta go."

I stuffed my bra in my back pocket and pulled my sweater over my lopsided hair, running my fingers through my twists to unflatten them. I bent down to give her a kiss and smelled my pussy on her lips. I smiled and kissed her deeply.

"I'll call you later. *I love you.*"

ૡ

Yawning as I walked out of my English literature class, I realized I really needed to get a full night's sleep beforehand or that man would put me to sleep. How could any professor be so oblivious to the intensity of their own monotony? *Got a Ph.D. but can't teach worth shit. How did he have tenure at New York University? Is this what my tuition and fees are paying for?* I entered the hall into a stream of students changing classes, all walking in multiple directions. Snippets of half-conversations floated across the hall. Distracted by my thoughts, I nearly ran into someone as I turned the corner.

"Oh! I'm sor—"

"What's up, Taylor?" Mike said.

"Nothin, just got out of class with Peters." I deliberately yawned to show him what I meant.

He laughed and turned around to walk in the direction I was going. "I told you to drop that class unless you wanted to spend the semester trying *not* to fall asleep."

"And I told you I *have* to, I need it for my major—you know the English department ain't trying to let anyone graduate without learning that classic white lit shit. Speaking of which, why am I majoring in English again?" I rolled my eyes. "Oh! Before I forget, are the flyers for A.C.'s show ready for pickup?"

He stopped dead in his tracks and looked at me, as if bracing himself. "Shit, Taylor, I didn't drop the flyers off."

"Mike—" I exhaled, disappointed. *Dis idjot* …

"I'm so sorry…"

"We need those flyers *now*. The performance is in seven days and nobody knows about it!"

"I didn't have time to drop them off." *Oh, please, not with this 'I was busy' shit again. Why why why people always decide they too busy to do shit after they said they could?*

"Why didn't you tell me? I could've done it," I said.

"I just didn't have time. I'm sorry." *You didn't have the time to drop it off or you didn't have the ten seconds it would've taken to call me to tell me you couldn't do it?*

"Do you have a copy of the flyer on you?" I asked, exasperated but trying to sound calm. I realized that going through his excuses was taking up valuable time I could be using to fix the situation.

"Let me see …" he said as he started digging through his duffel bag. He pulled out a crumpled copy of a flyer. No way could I photocopy that. I looked at it, then at him. "Do you have it saved on a jump drive?"

"Yeah."

"Do you have it with you?"

"Wait a minute ... Here you go—"

Make I hear word. I sucked my teeth in annoyance and snatched it from his hand. "Thanks. See you later."

"I need that back by tonight!"

I walked away, muttering, "Shit, I needed those flyers last week, but whatever."

I rushed to the third floor and into the computer room. Even though it was early, the room was full of people checking their email, finishing assignments and engaging in online bidding wars for famous people's underwear or whatever it is people spend their money on. I just needed one computer for two minutes. Sighing heavily, I impatiently shifted my weight. *Please don't let this be one of those days, it's only 11 a.m.* Laughter came from the opposite corner of the room, followed by the sound of rapid typing and, seconds later, more laughter. *Why is this moron chatting online? Hasn't he got classes? Homework? His* own *computer?*

I had to wait 10 more minutes before a computer was free. *Finally.* I sat down and stuck in the jump drive. *Please don't do anything funky to me.* It occurred to me that I didn't know what he'd named the file. Hopefully it wouldn't be named some random, stupid shit that I'd never guess. Searching through the contents of his disk, I came across term papers, miscellaneous graphics, music files and then, finally, "Poetry Flyer." I opened it and pressed print.

Seeing that the flyer was good eased my anger a teeny bit. *At least he got that part right.* It had white letters on a black background with a picture of A.C. in the center and these words beneath:

a poet's fist is mightier than any gun,
be:cause
it is at the drop of her words
that revolution is done.
Fri, January 27, 7pm,
Kimmel, Eisner & Lubin Auditorium
$10. All proceeds to Chinua Achebe High School

Okay, what shit do I have to do? Gotta grab lunch, call the printers, gotta go check out that book for my paper (shit that's due tomorrow!), gotta go to work at 5. Alright, alright. I knew I needed to update the other members of Diaspora Soul. I sent a rushed email to DS members:

```
Yo. Flyers didn't get printed yet. Am working on it. Please do word of mouth, tell EVERYBODY you know. TWICE. Xiomahra, could you send out a formal email to the poets of color student organization? Shauna, could you please hit up the prison abolitionists org? Tati, could you send out an email over the gender studies listserv? I ain't got time to do it. I've attached the flyer Mike made; please include it in your emails. Thanks y'all.

Peace.
*T.
```

As I rushed out, I slipped my phone from the back pocket of my jeans and called the printers. Sean was the only person I knew down there who I was cool with and *might* be able to pull this job off in a hurry as a favor.

"Copy Cat," a perky voice answered. "How may I help you?"

"Is Sean Demetri in?"

"No, he's not. He's away from the office—" *shit* "all day today." *shitshit* "Would you like to leave a message?"

"Uhh, no, thanks. If I dropped off a flyer, is there any way that you could make 700 copies of it by tomorrow?"

"What paper size?"

"8½ by 11 inches."

"Is it in color?"

"Yes."

"Usually, yes, but today we have a lot of orders and by the time we get to yours, it'll probably be late tomorrow. Chances are it'd be done by Monday afternoon."

The performance is next Friday. The performance is next Friday. The performance is next Friday.

"Hello?"

"I'm still here. Is there any way to put a rush on an order and possibly get it done sooner?"

"For an order that size it would be an extra $75. We'd get it done by Sunday morning." Great, too bad we don't have that $75 in our budget. Still gotta raise another $200 for the expenses already allocated in our existing budget. *Think, Queen, think.*

"Why don't you bring your flyer in right now and I'll see what we can do," she said.

"Alright, I'll be over in a few minutes. Thanks so much."

"No problem."

As I walked the few short blocks to Copy Cat, I fumed. We'd been working on getting this sista to campus for two months—how could we not have flyers done the week before the damn performance? How did that happen? A.C. was a writer, social critic and prison abolitionist. Her activism focused on getting incarcerated Black women free legal services to appeal their cases and overturn unjust convictions.

I hope the printers can hook this up. I pushed open the doors to their office, and tried to be optimistic.

The sound in the cramped space formed a sonic collage of chinging, clinging and occasional clicking. I scanned the room for someone to talk to. There were busy-looking people scattered all over, intently bent over machines. A woman walked in from a connecting room.

Damn.

She was mocha brown with cornrows on each side of her head that were braided up into an afro pompadour. Her hairstyle was Grace Jones-level fierce and her clothes perfectly accentuated even the subtlest of her curves.

Please turn around.

She saw me, put a long index finger up and mouthed the words "one minute." As if she'd heard my command, she turned around and returned to the room from which she had just come. She wore a cowl-neck sweater that looked fuzzy and warm. And she redefined the word "booty" in jeans that clung tightly to every curve.

Focus, Taylor.

I am, said the other dyke inside me. *I'm focused on her ass.* I smiled at my sexy, nasty sense of humor.

She returned with a stack of papers that she placed on someone's desk, then she made her way toward me.

"Hi, I'm sorry," she said. "How may I help you?" I wondered if she could read my thoughts.

"I don't know if it was you I talked to on the phone …"

I couldn't help but glance quickly down to where the rim of her sweater formed a crescent. The stretchy material clung to her breasts so beautifully. I noticed her colors and smiled. *Amen for that.* Never did red, orange, yellow, green, blue and violet beads look so good than hanging on a simple silver chain around her neck, clinging snugly to the base of her throat.

"Nice colors," I said.

"Thanks …" she said slowly. "You family?" She smiled, dimples diving into her cheeks.

I laughed. "Hell yeah, girl!" I relaxed, forgetting what I was there for.

"Where your colors at?"

"My shit beam so bright, I don't need no flag and I don't need no colors," I replied.

"Alright now," she said, and smiled. *Ouu.* Her smile was too warm for words. And those eyes ... Woo! I missed flirting. Her lip gloss was beaming messages to me.

"I think I've seen you around. You do poetry, right?" she said.

"Yeah."

"I saw you perform last night. That was a really powerful poem."

"Oh, thank you," I said. "I don't think I've seen you around campus."

"How could you miss me?" she asked playfully.

"I have no idea." I said, and smiled.

"Because I definitely didn't miss you," she said sweetly. I looked at her lips as they formed the word "you."

Are you hittin on me? my eyes asked.

What you think? hers replied.

My heart fluttered. Why is my heart fluttering? I have a girlfriend, I'm not supposed to get attracted to other women!

"What year are you?" I asked.

"Junior."

"I'm a sophomore," I said.

"I'm Sy."

"Taylor," I said. "Was it you I talked to on the phone?"

"Probably, I'm the phone diva around here. Your poem talked about ... a Nigerian river goddess ... You're Nigerian, oui?"

"Oui, tu es Africaine aussi?"

"Oui, je suis du Cameroun. Ah, tu parles français?"

"Un peu. Quelque fois. Lorsque mon esprit se souvient."

She laughed.

"We're neighbors," I said.

"Oui, oui. Alors, you're the one who wanted to put a rush on an order?"

I tensed a bit, remembering. "Yeah, that's me."

"Can I see the flyer?"

"Oh sure." I handed it to her.

"This is happening next Friday?"

"Yeah."

"I can see why you need to put a rush on it. All in color, 8½ by 11?"

"Yes."

"Honestly, girl, we got so much to do here, if you were to put in your order right now, we wouldn't get to it until tomorrow."

I sighed and rubbed my eyes.

"There's no way it could get started today?" I asked, hoping for a "yes" but dreading a "no." *This is the last time I let Mike do* anything *that requires a due date.*

"Well …" her voice trailed off. "I'm trying to think of when a machine will be free. Hmm, his order should be done in an hour," she said to herself. "… I could put yours on then … 700 copies won't take more than half an hour but then we'd get even more behind. Shit … okay, okay, how about this: I'll do your order after hours when we're closed, that way all the machines will be free and I won't be putting you ahead of anybody and nothing will get delayed."

"You could do that?"

"Sure."

"Doesn't that mean you'd have to stay overtime?"

"Uh-huh," she said simply.

"Thank you *so* much."

"Please, girl, anything for fam." She winked. "We close at 6:30. I can start it at 6:45 when everyone's gone. I'm locking up since Sean's not here today, so I'll just stay late. It should be done by 7:30 at the latest. Could you email me the actual file by 6 today? The quality of your flyers will be much better if I use the original file rather than a copy of a printout."

"I have it on a jump drive right here." I took off my messenger bag and reached in to find it. "The file is called 'Poetry Flyer' and it's in a folder called 'Graphics.' Mike used Photoshop to create it and the resolution is really high so I'm hoping it'll be fine."

"Thank you," she said, taking the drive from me.

"Oh, and I work from 5 to 7, so I won't be able to be here with you the whole time."

"That's okay, I can handle it," she teased.

I smiled. "I'll come by when I get off work to pick them up. Thanks so much, Sy. I really appreciate this. I know you don't have to do this. Will you get in trouble?"

"It's no problem, don't worry bout me. Just breathe and handle your business."

"Thank—"

"Stop with the gushin and be out. You got five million things to do, right?"

I nodded.

"So go do em." *If I could put you on my to-do list, I would, girl.* Where'd that unnecessarily lustful thought come from?

"Ai'ight, peace."

Praise Goddess! What kind of beauty just happened? I breathed in and out, really happy for the first time since my conversation with Mike, beginning to believe that everything might actually work out just fine.

☙❧

I knocked on the door to Copy Cat at a quarter after 7. Sy opened the door with a smile.

"What's up?"

"Nothin, just happy to be off work."

"Where you work?"

"I clean my professor's house every week," I said.

"You look tense."

"I do?"

"Uh-huh. Didn't I tell you to breathe earlier?"

"I did," I said defensively.

"Try taking deeper breaths then."

I laughed, relaxing a little.

"I guess I just have a lot on my mind."

"Like what?" she asked.

"Organizing this event, homework, regular everyday stress. Plus, I'm always a little tense when I leave cleaning because it takes so much energy."

"After we're done, you need to go sit somewhere and relax."

"Can't, I gotta put up these flyers once they're done printing."

Her jaw dropped. "That can't wait till tomorrow?"

"Nope. We only have seven days to let the campus know A.C.'s coming. Gotta start now."

"Taylor." She said my name like it was a statement, like my mama does when she's about to scold me. "I'm taking you out for hot chocolate at Sweeter after these flyers are done."

"What?"

"You need to relieve something. You're too tense."

"But I gotta put—"

"Aren't there other people working on this?"

"Yeah, I'ma drop off some flyers at their doors so they can put them up."

"No."

"What?" I was confused; I hadn't asked her a question that required a yes or no response.

"No," she said again. "That's too much legwork. You're going to put up flyers tonight *and* drop flyers off at *how* many people's rooms?"

Mentally, I counted. "Five."

"Oh, hell no. Legwork increases stress; the more running

around you do, the more stressed out you're likely to get. Why don't you make them come get the flyers from you? Like ... put them in a box outside your door and have them picked up. Email or call to let them know they're ready and they can come get them."

I looked at her like she was a new species I was watching on the Discovery Channel. How did she just drop that knowledge in twenty seconds?

"Damn, that's a good idea."

"I know Black women are strong, but shit, that doesn't mean we gotta do every single thing for every damn body all the fuckin time. If you don't have your cell phone, there's phones all over the office; feel free to use one. They'll be done in a few minutes and then you can drop them off at your room if you want."

At 7:30 on the dot, the flyers were done. I breathed deeply, relieved. I divided the flyers into six equal bundles so each of us organizers could have one. I wrapped a huge rubber band around each bundle, then texted my fellow organizers asking them to pick up a bundle from a box outside my dorm room door.

Progress.
Exhale.

ʚɞ

After dropping the flyers off, I met Sy back at Copy Cat. We hopped on a Brooklyn-bound train, and rode inside the roaring, rickety belly of the city to Sweeter, a fly little coffee shop in Fort Greene that I hadn't been to since last semester. Upstairs in the café they were playin soulful old school Chaka Khan on a "Sweet Thang" tip. We sat facing each other over a tiny round table, the rim of which was lined with little strings of midnight blue beads that jingled whenever either of us moved. The overhead lighting was dark blue, and short, thick, indigo candles lit up each table.

"I work here on the weekends," Sy said.

"Really? My homie, Tatiyana, works here, too."

"Did somebody say mi nombre?"

"Tati!" I got up and hugged her. "How are you?"

"Good, love," Tati said, her self-described café con un poquito de leche skin beaming. Her hair was in spaghetti-thin, charcoal-black microbraids and piled into a bun on the crown of her head. She wore a loose, sleeveless white T, jeans and high tops. Tati and Sy exchanged cheek kisses.

"Tatiyana and I both work the day shift on Saturday," Sy said.

"Good to see you, Tay! We need to kick it soon." Tati's tongue ring sparkled in her mouth as she spoke; her long eyelashes framed her warm, brown eyes.

"Most definitely," I said. She affectionately caressed my shoulder.

Tati took our orders then whisked off to the next table.

"Sooo," I said. "You work here *and* at the print shop? *And* go to NYU?"

"Yes, I work at the print shop during the week and here on the weekends."

"When do you find time for school?"

"I'm part-time at NYU this year," she explained. "Last year was … intense. I needed to give myself time to breathe. So I cut my class load in half."

"Damn. Stop hogging all the African immigrant stereotypes."

"What you mean? Ohh—me having mad jobs?"

"Yeah," I said sarcastically.

"Abeg, how I go eat, sef?"

"*Na wa o!* You sabi Pidgin?" I asked, surprised.

"I speak am small small."

I raised my palms above my head, reaching for the sky on the other side of the ceiling.

"My heart dey sing afrobeat praise song oooo." I clapped my hands in a joyous polyrhythmic melody. "Where did you learn?"

"Nollywood movies," she said, and we both laughed. "And my first lover was Nigerian. When she was mad … or coming … she spoke Pidgin. In Cameroon, we speak some of the same Pidgin as you—oh, and my mom sometimes speaks Naija Pidgin. So that's the sum total of my Pidgin education. And trust me, if I didn't *have* to have two jobs, I wouldn't. Anyway … how many jobs *you* got?"

"Two—"

"Case. In. Point. What they say in tennis? Set—match?"

"Shut uppp," I said, and laughed.

"You didn't know I'm double majoring in neuroscience and endocrinology?"

"I know, right?" I smiled. "Africans immigrate here and don't just get *any* education. No, no, they need to master *the* most complicated sciences. But what's your major, for real?"

"Political science with a minor in photography. Et toi?"

"English." I rolled my eyes. "For now. I'm considering minoring in Africana Studies."

Tati came back with mugs filled with hot cocoa topped with whipped cream. I wrapped my palms around my mug, letting the warmth flow into me.

"What are you thinkin about?" Sy asked after Tati left. The candle flame flickered slightly with her breath.

I took a swallow of my cocoa. It slid down my throat, warming my entire chest.

"How good this cup feels … and trying to figure out a way to thank you for all you did for me today."

"I know exactly how you can thank me."

"How?"

"Take me out to dinner." She smiled.

"Sy … I have a girlfriend."

"Oh." She paused for a second. "So take me out anyway."

"Ai'ight, just as long as you know I'm taken."

"Thank you for the heads up. We can do that friendship shit I keep hearing so much about."

Laughter danced out of me to the same flirtatious beat of the butterflies in my belly. "When you free?" I asked.

"The night after tomorrow."

"7 p.m.?"

"Sure."

"Where do you want to eat?"

Sy smiled slyly. "Surprise me."

I liked how carefree she was.

"So …" she began. "What do you do besides run around all day fixing the fuck-ups of fellow activists?"

I burst into laughter, almost choking on my hot chocolate.

"Quoi?" she asked sweetly.

"Oh my—! I can't believe you just said that!"

"C'est vrai, n'est-ce pas?" she asked.

"I think I'm supposed to be offended that you said that."

"Pourquoi?"

"Because Mike is my friend."

"I didn't say anything about his ability to be a good friend," Sy said. "Anyway tell me about A.C. Why are you bringing her here?"

"Well, the performance is a fundraiser for the independent, arts-based, Pan Africanist high school she's starting in Oakland. The learning will be based on the work of amazing African and Black folks globally. She sent me the syllabus for one of the classes: Queer African Diasporic Lit. Shit, I want to take that class. So Diaspora Soul, the organization I co-chair with my homie, Xio, is bringing her just because she's amazing." I gushed. "A.C.'s about some real shit. She's co-founder of I Didn't Do It, Inc., an organization that works to get wrongly convicted Black women out of prison. Several of the women whose convictions she worked to have overturned are now working in the *same* organization side by side with A.C. trying to exonerate other women. It's this beautiful, reciprocal circle where folks can come out of prison and immediately turn their gratitude for someone caring about *their* case into them caring about someone else's."

"That's what's up!"

"Exactly."

"So Diaspora Soul—what do you do?"

"DS organizes events that address political and social issues that impact queer immigrants and queer children of immigrants. We mostly bring artists to campus so they can share how they use their artwork to explore their politics and identity. A.C.'s work is so in line with why we created DS in the first place. I admire her because she's more than just talk and she doesn't follow trends, not even the trends in the quasi-revolutionary, young, Black, militant clique of artist/activists. And she's also a really great poet."

"She sounds like my new favorite shero. I don't think I've read or heard any of her stuff, but when I saw the flyer she looked familiar."

"She was on the cover of *The Village Voice* a couple weeks ago."

"For real? For what?"

"Even though she's based out of Oakland, she was collaborating with that independent charter school in Bed-Stuy, that's doing grassroots fundraising for their own Pan Africanist elementary school."

"Damn, I think I might have heard about that—supposedly 'at-risk' Brooklyn youth raised thousands of dollars from their community when no one thought it was possible because, what did the article say? Oh, oh yeah, the community is so 'economically depressed.' She sounds really fierce. Is she a dyke?"

"Of course!" We laughed. "*And* she's Nigerian."

"Uh-oh! West Africa in the house!"

1884

Even though she lived in Bed-Stuy, Sy rode the train twenty minutes back to Manhattan with me. She said she needed a book for a class assignment due the next morning, so she insisted on walking me home and, um, I really didn't protest. We stood in front of my political statement-covered door. I had both my flags up—my Nigerian one and my gay pride one. We briefly hugged and for that moment, my palms spanned her back.

As we pulled apart, Sy smiled and pointed at the "My Uterus, My Choice" bumper sticker taped to my door. "Hell, yes!" Sy read off one of my posters: "'African Dykes Stand Up!' Yes, yes, yes! I thought you said you didn't have any pride gear?"

"I had to put some on my door because my hall is so straight, it's painful sometimes."

She laughed. "This image is so intense," she said. Her fingertips caressed the poster; in it, two African women in traditional dress kissed each other in the marketplace. One woman had a woven basket filled with green plantain on her head; the other had a baby tied to her back. The image was framed by an outline of the African continent with the words "African Dykes Stand Up!" beneath in graffiti letters.

"That's my favorite pride poster."

"I love African women," Sy said. Wonderment colored her voice, as if sharing an intimate thought out loud. I loved that her voice deepened when she said it.

I leaned against the wall beside my door, pressing my palms into its coolness. "Did you immigrate here or were you born in the States?" I asked.

"I was born in Cameroon and moved to the U.S. when I was 15."

"Where?"

"Harlem."

"My family moved from Nigeria to Vermont before I was born," I said. "What ethnicity—"

"I'm Fulani. And you're …?"

"Urhobo. There's Fulanis in Nigeria, too!"

"I know. That's what happens when white men get together and randomly divide our continent. Ethnic groups get separated by a line on a map." Sy sucked her teeth, annoyed.

"I remember sitting in my first ever anthropology class," I said. "It was my first year of college, and hearing about that conference in Berlin where Europe divided up Africa like—"

"Those racist bastards sat around a table and figured out which European countries would colonize which African territories."

"Exactly. Africa is *still* feeling the effects of that shit."

"The year was 1884," she said. "That date is burned into my memory. That conference is why I speak French, why my name is Syrus Rêve Devereux and not Madiko Manga or a name that's in my own precious language."

"That conference is why my name is Taylor, which most of the time I'm fine with. If I had an Urhobo first name, I don't know if I'd have the energy to deal with my first *and* last name being butchered every single day," I said. "But … there are days that I want my name to be … Odaro. Odaro Ejiroghene."

"I started taking photographs because they *transcend* language. Language can only go so far. There's that place that words just can't touch, you know what I mean?"

"I do, I do. Writing can feel like constantly trying to describe what can't be described. Like … like how it feels to be *home* in Nigeria after having been away, how the air feels, what it's like to have my little brother run up to me and hug me so hard when he's never affectionate."

I smiled, remembering.

I'd forgotten that memory.

I *love* that memory.

"That's magic. That's what love is," I said. "Can I capture that in a poem? I can try but—"

"It's never quite exactly right."

"I come close because I'm a good writer." I laughed. "But nothing can ever exactly capture that moment."

"A photograph of that hug between you and your brother—"

"—would come closer, of course, to bringing that feeling to life because of the visual element," I said.

"That's what I mean by photographs transcending language," Sy said. "Anyone who speaks any language could look at that photo and see your love for each other. Photographs say some of the things that can't fit into language. It frustrates me that we're even speaking in this white man English right now instead of in our mother tongues."

"That frustration is the story of my life, Sy. I love writing poems but sometimes I resent how much I can articulate these beautiful things in this language that I don't know how to say in Urhobo. I feel like English has choked my voice, choked what I sometimes think is my real voice. I don't know if I'll ever learn to express myself in my own language."

"Being in this country is not going to help any of us speak our mother tongues." We paused for a moment, breathing.

"So ... you're a photographer?" I asked.

Sy laughed. "Yes ma'am. What gave it away?"

"I don't know, maybe all the passionate speak about photography? Also, you told me it's your minor, remember? What do you photograph?"

"I take pictures about what you spit poems about. Photos are my way of writing poems, only my words are visual."

"That's … *wow.*"

"Sometimes words are just too much … and not enough, and make such a mess of things." Sy's eyes lit up, like light making an unexpected prism through glass. "I'm not that good with words, so photography is a way for me to talk in a different way."

"I think you're great with words," I said.

"Well, thank you. I've gotten better. But sometimes I can't find the *exact* words to express the *exact* thing I feel or think. In my head—" She brought her fingertips to her temples, closed her eyes and caressed her forehead like her fingers were sketching an image. "—I can see what I'm feeling as the perfect photograph but the words aren't there. That used to really annoy my ex."

Sy opened her eyes with a smile, returning my gaze.

"When you take photographs, is it around a certain theme or idea or do you just take pictures of whatever moves you without considering if it fits into a theme?"

"I'd say … both. I was in Cameroon last summer and I was so sad about how much I could feel and see of Europe and the States *in* Africa. I started taking photos of youth rockin jeans, perms in people's hair, the cigarette and Coca-Cola billboards everywhere … and that became my 1884 series, which I dedicated to my mom." Sy's voice was warm, her eyes softening as if recalling a fond memory. "She's a historian. She taught me about colonization, about 1884, and about African politics over breakfast every morning."

"It's the same in Nigeria with all the ads and the hair," I said.

"Of course it is. It makes me angry but mostly sad. I wanted to capture some of the effects of colonization that we don't always talk about in poli sci. We talk about the need for infrastructure in our countries, clean water and how we need to control our own natural resources since we were robbed of that during colonization, and of course that's important. But there are other effects that go deeper than that, that are about how we see ourselves—like do we think we're beautiful?"

"And do we value, love, respect our traditional culture, our spirituality?" I asked. "Your art sounds profound, beautiful …

and heartbreaking all at the same time."

"That's how I feel as I take the photographs. It's such an intense release to capture something beautiful and sacred in one moment of time." She paused, contemplating. "I'm sorry, you probably have to get to bed. I could talk all night about art and Africa. Those are my two first loves."

"You and me both. Please don't apologize. Do you do self-portraits?"

"Never."

"Never?" I asked.

"I find comfort in *not* being in the spotlight. That's why I'm a photographer. I like to lay back in the cut a little."

"Would you ever let yourself be photographed?"

"Like, professionally?"

"Yeah … by an artist who maybe wanted to put you in a series of their own."

She thought for a second. "No. I don't think I would."

"So your 1884 series … do you think Africans shouldn't wear jeans and have perms? What's the message behind the series?"

"You're the poet, remember? I'm a photographer, so it'll make the most sense when you see it. It's not that I have a problem with Africans wearing jeans; we're both Africans who are rockin jeans right now. As Africans, we maintain and retain a lot of our authentic African culture, *and* we create new parts of our culture all the time. What my series focuses on is that a lot of African culture is changed and influenced by European and American culture, like what clothes we wear. And our breathtaking Cameroonian landscape is so often littered with billboards for European products that are not good for us—soda, cigarettes, liquor—all with smiling Africans, smiling as they consume these poisonous, unhealthy products. That make sense?"

"Yes, it does. I wanna see your work!"

"Anytime, anytime. You're more than welcome to come

over. I'm blessed to have a small darkroom in my apartment, so I'm constantly developing new photos."

"Thank you for every—"

"Oh, stop it with the thank yous, sista."

"But—"

"Shhh," she said. She put a finger on my lips and looked at me. "Dimanche à sept heures, oui?"

I nodded.

She smells like jasmine.

"Bonne nuit, Odaro." My heart blushed and fluttered a little.

"Madiko." The softness in my voice mirrored hers. "Bonne nuit."

I watched her walk down the hall and turn the corner. When I unlocked my door, my alarm clock's red letters defiantly read "2:05 a.m." Fuck homework now, no way was I gonna stay up until 4 a.m. then wake up at 8 for my 9 a.m. kickboxing class. I'd just have to wake up early to do it … in theory. It's a never-ending tug of war for college students: work or sleep? Sleep or work?

I chose sleep this time.

FOR SIZAKELE

plantain

Lee breezed into the kitchen of her apartment. "Baby, you making plátanos?"

"No," I answered, hips cradling the top of the oven door. "I'm making *plantain*."

"What?" she asked, confused. She grabbed a glass from the cupboard next to my head and poured water into it. "It's the same thing."

"No, it's not."

She gulped down water. "Yeah, it is."

"It's really not. That's the Spanish word for plantain."

"Exactly."

"I'm not Latina."

"What's that got to do with anything?" Lee placed her glass on the counter.

"I mean that *plátanos*, as a word, has no cultural significance to me, which it might if I was Latina or Xicana or from a diaspora of folks who speak Spanish. How many times do I have to tell you that they're not plátanos to me?"

"Ain't you the one always talking about the diaspora of this, that, and the other people and how we're all more connected than we think?"

"Yeah, I'm also always talking about *misnaming*. We're obviously connected; all you have to do is eat our food to see where we overlap. But I can't call plantain 'plátanos,' because that's not what they are to me. It would be like translating my last name into another language."

"It's just one word. Don't you think you could be overanalyzing this just a *little* bit?"

"Nope," I said flatly. "Why do Black folks always wanna say plátanos? Why not say it in Twi? Or in Yorùbá? But no, it has to be in Spanish because Spanish is this hypersexualized language."

"It could also be because some Black people are Latino too or it could be that so many of us grew up around Latinos and therefore the Spanish language. Taylor, I really don't see what the big deal is."

"Lee, could you *please* just call it what I call it? It's hard enough for me to cook these for you," I said. My words fell heavily into the sizzling frying pan.

"So, is English the language of the Urhobo people?"

"Of course not. I mean, we can speak it but our language is Urhobo."

"Plantain is an English word, so what's the difference between calling it a Spanish word and an English word?"

Shit, I never thought of it like that. I stopped mid-motion, holding two raw slices of plantain in my hand, suspended over the sizzling oil. It *is* an English word. As a teenager in Nigeria, my beloved grandmother had taught me how to fry plantain as she told me stories about my mama in the most beautiful Pidgin. With Broken English more complete than any unbroken, standard version, she had shown me how to slice plantain the long way to produce oval-shaped pieces and how to heat the corn oil until just the right moment and then slide the raw plantain slices into the pan gently so the hot oil didn't splash onto me.

Lee added, "If it's so important to call it the right name, why don't you say it in Urhobo?"

I regained motion and tossed two plantain slices into the frying pan with a resentfulness that had been brewing in me for the last few years. Reticence stitched my words to the inside of my mouth.

"Because I don't know how to speak Urhobo."

Yet.

After we ate, Lee washed dishes. As she scrubbed the greasy frying pan, she laughed. "I feel like you're a dyke in the meantime," Lee said, her hands covered in soapsuds.

I didn't even know how to respond to that.

"What's that supposed to mean?"

"You're bi, Taylor. You can slip in and out of both worlds. You have a choice."

Yeah, I have a choice like pick my favorite ovary. Whatever.

"How do I have a choice?" I asked.

"I just said how."

"Oh, okay. So I guess that makes you more oppressed than me?"

"I didn't say that, but you don't understand half the shit dykes go through."

"Well, then, tell me what I don't understand, Lee. Why don't you explain it to me?"

"If you don't know, I can't tell you."

"Thanks for that cryptic, fuckin non-answer," I said. I moved next to her and began drying the dishes. I thought for a minute, then asked, "Is this about Ahsha?"

"What?"

"This attitude, this anger you have about bi women, about bi femme women?"

"How does this have *anything* to do with Ahsha?"

"The way I've heard you talk about her, it's like you blame her cheating on her being bi."

"How does that relate to me saying that you don't know what dykes like me go through?" Lee asked, her voice hardening.

"I think the attitude you're coming at me with right now is more about Ahsha than me, which isn't fair. That's for one. Two, you have no right to tell me I can choose my sexuality—it's like you're making my experience less significant than yours. Even if I was choosing to be bi—so the fuck what? I'm a dyke. And three … I don't think you'd be comin out your face at me like this if I was a butch lesbian."

"You're right, I wouldn't, because I wouldn't be dating you and we wouldn't be having this conversation."

I rolled my eyes. "You're missing my point."

"Taylor, stop trying to psychoanalyze me. This is *not* about Ahsha."

"Maybe it's about another one of your exes, because I *know* it's not about me. I've never done anything even remotely close to cheating on you so I know you're punishing me for the sins of someone who came before me."

"I didn't say anything about you cheating on me." She rinsed her hands, then sat down on the window ledge.

"You didn't have to; I know where this conversation is going. First, you start talking shit about me being bisexual, as if that shit is brand new, like you haven't known I'm bi since we met. Then you make some comment about how I don't understand your butch struggle. *Then* you accuse me of cheating or tell me you expect me to. Your complaints are predictable."

"They're predictable to you because you're always putting the same words in my mouth," Lee snapped.

"I'm really fuckin sick of this Lee. If the shit your exes did still bothers you, then call them, talk about it, get angry, but direct it toward *them,* not me. We've been together for a year and I still hear this bullshit. If you have an issue with bisexual women, why do you date them? And why are you with me when you're clearly not over your ex?"

"I'm *over* Ahsha. You're the one who's not over her. You act jealous."

"Maybe you don't love her anymore, but you still hate what she did … and with a passion that makes you expect I'll do what she did just cuz she and I both happen to be bisexual. Would you like me to get upset at you for what the butches I dated before you did to me? That seems like a logical way to have a healthy relationship, right?"

"Of course I hate what she did. I came home and found her fuckin my homeboy in our bed. But all of this shit you're bringing up isn't the point."

"You're right—you snappin on me for some shit some other dyke did isn't the point. The fact that you keep taking your anger out on me for things I haven't even done isn't the point. What is the fuckin point then?"

"The point is that you act like you're a dyke and you're not—"

My jaw dropped. She stopped, eyes wide, apologetic, knowing even before I said a word that her words had hurt me.

Her voice melted in regret. "Baby, I'm sor—"

"I'm not a what, Lee?"

"Taylor—"

"I didn't hear you, Lee." My voice dripped sarcasm.

"I didn't mean it like—"

"Yes, you did. You just didn't mean to say it out loud," I said. I dried my hands on a dishrag, then threw it angrily onto the counter. I started storming out of the kitchen, but Lee said something that made me pause: "Walking away is easy."

I let her speak to my back, my arms defiantly folded across my chest.

"Why are you so heated? I mean, *really.* Is it because of the dyke thing? Or is it because I said something a little too true earlier? English *is* just as much a language used to colonize as Spanish. And unless you tell people you're bi, you *are* exempt from a lot of the shit butch dykes like me have to go through because you pass for straight. You know this. Why are you angry at me for saying the shit?"

My nostrils flared slightly as I closed my eyes and sighed. I icily turned to face her, then let her see the ice in my eyes melt and turn into weariness.

"I shouldn't have to prove myself to you. Just because our struggles aren't the same doesn't make either one more difficult than the other. What do you think it feels like to hear you, my woman, say these words to me? You, who are supposed to understand me. You, who should always have my back. You're the one telling me that somehow my day-to-day struggle as a dyke is not as hard as yours. This right here, *this right here*—" I said, making a circle with my hands encompassing her and I "—is a big part of my day-to-day struggle: having to constantly make other dykes recognize my pain. You think it's easy passing? Do you know how many fucked up things I hear *because* I pass?"

"Do you know how much fucked up shit I hear because I *don't* pass, Taylor?"

"Yes, actually I *do*, because when you tell me I *listen* and I *believe* you. I have never second-guessed you when you talk about the bullshit you go through. I sympathize and comfort you through it, Lee. Do you remember all the stories you've come home and told me? And how I've supported you through all that? Every time you called me pissed off, or emailed me some fucked up shit someone said or did, I always tried my fuckin hardest to be a refuge to you from that. People get comfortable and let their bigotry spew out their mouth because they think I'm 'one of them' in ways that they don't in front of you because you come off as butch and people know you're a dyke just by looking at you. I have to go out of my way to be rainbowed down if I want other dykes to know I'm a dyke just by looking at me. All you have to do is walk into a room and women salivate because they *know*."

It was getting tiring having to make itemized lists of my oppression to get taken seriously.

"In case you hadn't noticed, I don't just let myself pass. I out myself every single day, over and over, so all those assholes who thought I was one of them have to deal with my dyke ass checkin them on their heterosexist, homophobic, transphobic shit."

"Alright, yes, it's important that you check people on their shit. But Taylor, every single day I walk out the door and, just by dressing the way that's most comfortable to me, people stare at me like I'm a sideshow. Yes, it's dope when other dykes recognize me and I recognize them, but when straight people recognize me, too, it's like I'm a car accident they can't take their eyes off of. I'm a glitch in their matrix, a freak of nature and I'm horrifying yet so fuckin entertaining. Everywhere I go, I can feel people's eyes on me. It makes me feel nasty. When you walk down the street, Taylor, you don't deal with the shit I do."

"And when *you* walk down the street, baby, you don't deal with the shit that *I have to.* From creepy dudes following me down the street trying to holla, to always feelin like I need to be ready to defend myself against attack."

"They look at me like I'm not a woman," Lee said. "Like I must want to be a man. Some men are intimidated and some feel like they can look down on me because to them, beneath it all, I'm just another bitch anyway. As for women, there are the closeted ones who are curious about me and then there are the ultra-hyper-super-straight ones who are scared *of* me because they assume I want them. None of them, though, ever look at me like I'm just a woman buying some damn groceries who happens to be wearing baggy clothes. I'm an 'other.' You have the privilege of being a woman and passing for 'normal.'"

"Is it a privilege now?"

"I'm talking about your humanity. You're a *woman*, I'm an 'other.' I'm something people can't understand, some *thing* they can't categorize."

Neither of us said anything for a moment.

"That's really fucked up, Lee. It really is. I want you to see what I'm going through, too. I love saying I'm femme even though I know it's a fuckin category, but sometimes it just gets in the way of who I really am. Once I say I'm femme, I'm expected to represent all of what that's supposed to be, even if all that is femme isn't all that I am. Labels keep us from being *us,* keep us busy living up—or down—to what that label is. On top of that, we find ways to fight each other over who's the most oppressed. There are tons of stories I have tucked under my tongue, scared to share with you, because I'm sure you'll blow off what I have to say just as easily as you blew off me being a fuckin dyke. I *am* a dyke, whether you agree with me or not, whether I'm attracted to men or not. Because I know so in my soul and *because I fuckin say so*. I don't need anyone's validation to know that. It would just be nice to get that from you, because how you see me *matters* to me."

Lee leaned against the windowpane behind her and was silent for several moments. I wondered if our conversation was over. Even though I'd tried hard to articulate how I felt, I wondered if it had made any difference in how she understood me.

"I want you to feel like you can tell me any and all of your stories," Lee said softly." I'm sorry for saying you're not a dyke. It's not even my place to tell you what you can call yourself and … I won't call your plantain 'plátanos'." Lee paused. "I don't have the best history, herstory as you'd say, with bi women, so sometimes I think that clouds how I see you."

"Thank you," I said quietly. "I'm sorry for snapping at you." I unfolded my arms and walked closer to her.

"All that anger wasn't necessarily about you," I admitted. "I just get tired of feeling like I have to prove I'm a dyke and I really can't deal with having that between us. I am so fiercely protective of the parts of my culture that I know about, that something that seems as simple as plantain is … not so simple to me. It's the heartbeat of who I am. Whether we're talking about plantain or language or colonizers fuckin with my people's land, it's all the same to me. Every injury is a big one or is connected to something else, and that's why something that seems so small to you upsets me so much … and I'm sorry for taking all that out on you."

She stepped closer to me and placed her hands on my waist. "Is it really hard to cook plantain for me?"

I thought a moment. "Only when I feel like you're not seeing or respecting my culture for what it is: African. Then I feel like I'm explaining who I am to you as I cook and it hurts when I don't feel like you're hearing me."

"That's not what I meant to do. I was joking about the dyke thing; I didn't mean for my joke to hurt you."

"But that *is* what you think, though—that I'm not a dyke because I'm bi?"

"Well … yeah, but—"

"Then it's not a joke then," I said. I was getting heated all over again.

"Baby, it's what I think. I ain't gonna lie to you. But I think I need to re-think what I think. Because maybe my ass is wrong."

I breathed in and out slowly, calming myself, letting myself hear her words. "Thank you for saying that, baby."

"Of course." She squeezed my ass affectionately.

"Plus, you know I don't be cooking for just *anybody.*"

She smiled. "I appreciate you cooking and … I don't like to fight but I *love* this part."

"What part?"

"Making up."

"Oh, is that what this is?" I asked.

"I hope so, otherwise I wasted an apology."

"Really?" Lee saw the beginning of annoyance on my face. Her words tumbled out: "Just playin, just playin. You know I apologized and I meant it."

"Hmmm," I grumbled with a half-smile.

"Tay, baby?"

"Uh-huh?" I whispered, then slid my hand under her shirt, over her belly.

"I love you," she said.

I gobbled up all her words in my kiss.

⁂

After basketball practice, Lee tried to sneak into her bedroom without waking me. I sleepily opened my eyes to a room coated in the blackness of night, then looked over at the clock. 1:09 a.m.

"Baby … who practices till one in the morning?"

"Someone really dedicated. Sorry, I was trying not to wake you."

I heard her groan. I sat up in bed and turned on the bedside lamp.

"You sore?"

"Yes."

"You in pain?"

"Yeah."

"Come over here and take off all your clothes."

"Tay, I love you but I'm so tired—"

"*Please.* This is purely for your health."

She got undressed, and lay belly-down on the bed on top of our rumpled sheets. Sitting at the base of her back, I leaned down to melt a tender kiss between her shoulder blades. Her back was still damp with sweat. I sunk my fingers into her tense shoulders, crooning "relax, relax" as I carefully kneaded her neck and shoulders. Lee tried to talk over her shoulder.

"I know you have an early class tomorrow so you don't have to—"

"Lee, I *want* to."

"You'll be tired all day."

"And you'll be sore all day if I don't, so *shhhh.*"

☙❧

"CHRIIIIIISSSS!" Lee shouted. I woke up terrified, instinctively tightening my arms around Lee's sharp, fitful movements. Lee pushed at my stomach and kicked her legs. I wrapped my arms around her anyway.

"Chris! You can't, can't—"

"Lee, wake up, wake up! You're having a nightmare."

Lee alternated between screaming and mumbling.

"Lee babybaby, *calm down, calm down*—"

"Stop it, stop it!"

I shook her hard and said in a stern, commanding voice, "Lee, *wake up*."

Her breathing was heavy and jagged as if she'd been running miles. Her eyes were scared. She trembled, naked and disoriented.

"Love, I'm here, *shhhh*—" She pushed me away as she moved to get out of bed but my palm firmly caught the side of her hip.

"Don't run." She stopped. "Come here." She turned, jaw clenched, eyes deliberately avoiding mine. In a delicate voice, I murmured, "Can I hold you?"

She flared her nostrils then nodded slightly. I wrapped my arms around her with as much strength as I could muster, gather, summon and render. She didn't return my embrace.

"I love you," I said. She sighed heavily. I felt her chest shake with uneven breaths.

"Tay… I'm *sorry*—" She finally looked into my eyes and my heart broke from the pain I saw in hers.

"Don't be sorry. I'm here for you baby … *I love you*."

"How can you love me? When you know …"

"I love you because I love you. You're beautiful." She finally returned my embrace and laid her head in the crook of my neck in a way she rarely ever did. My arms tightened around her.

"I still have nightmares … after all these years. I can still feel him … on top of me …"

I tried to regulate my anger by breathing slowly in, and even slower out.

"I was 13."

"I know," I whispered. Since last Christmas when she'd told me about Chris, I'd wanted to know more but had been scared to say the wrong thing. So I waited. For her to choose what she wanted to tell me. And when.

"He …" She trembled, and although it hurt my heart, I let my body swallow the earthquakes of her pain. Lee wept in my arms so intensely that she shook and I shook with her. The rage in my chest was building and burning, rising and turning, images flashing through my mind with a frequency and vividness I couldn't control or make subside. Lee was once a 13-year-old girl growing up in Boston, a tomboy who loved to climb trees and play hide-and-go-seek, with dirt under her fingernails and skinned knees, who was always late for dinner because she was outside playing with the neighborhood kids. I couldn't even imagine how she had walked away from that terrifying violation, couldn't imagine if she'd returned to climbing trees and skinned knees afterward or if she'd retreated into a somber, taciturn world of her own making.

"It happened in the spring," she said. "I fuckin hate spring."

We lay there holding our breath, me holding her, my rage holding me, and the throbbing heartache in my chest as palpable as my thundering heartbeat.

ଓଃ

It was so early, too early to be doing anything but cuddling or dreaming, preferably both. The entire week I'd been up late and waking up with the sun. It was barely light outside and Lee's bedroom was tinged with a dark yellow, the sun peeking and leaking into the room through the edges of the balcony's curtain. I reached for Lee and grabbed blanket instead of body.

"I left your ticket on the kitchen counter," I heard her say from the adjoining bathroom.

"For—" I cleared my throat and tried again. "For what?"

Lee, clad in a white sports bra and red sweatpants, came to stand in the doorway between the bedroom and the bathroom.

"My basketball game. The big game I've been talking about and practicing till ridiculous hours in the night for."

Oh shit.

"It's tonight?"

Silence.

"Yes," she said, already sounding disappointed.

"I—"

"Can't make it?" Resentment coated her voice.

"I'm sorry, Lee, I didn't realize it was tonight. A.C.'s plane is coming in tonight and—"

"And you have other shit to do."

Of all the nights for there to be a conflict between our plans, *why tonight?* How could I not remember? This was becoming a habit with us, with me. I closed my eyes sadly.

"You know if I could be there, I would be."

"Actually, I *don't* know that. If it weren't this, it'd be something else."

"That's not true—"

"Yes, it is," she said calmly. "It's always something else that can't be avoided and 'shit, Lee, I'm sorry, next time I'll be there.' I'm running out of next times."

She returned to the bathroom, annoyed.

I walked into the kitchen and picked up the ticket on the counter. There was a sticky note attached:

"Take me out to dinner after the game? Love, L."

The game started at 8 p.m. A.C.'s plane got in at 8:45, and by the time I picked her up, collected her luggage, drove through traffic and got her settled into her hotel room, the game would be just about over.

She emerged from the bedroom fully dressed. "And I bet you need my car to pick her up, huh?"

Lee angrily threw the car keys onto the couch, grabbed her backpack from beside the coffee table and headed for the door.

"About last night—"

She turned back to face me. "What about it?"

"I don't know if you remember, but you had another night—"

"I don't wanna talk about that shit."

Door slam.
Fuck.

FOR SIZAKELE

sisí èkó

Driving soothed me; Brooklyn's streets shape-shifted into Queens' streets en route to JFK. The bright lights of the airport beamed in the night. My hands tightened and loosened the wheel as I envisioned Lee running onto the basketball court with her teammates, looking up to the stands for me out of habit and realizing all over again that I wasn't there. I sighed, realizing there was nothing I could do at that moment to make things right. I pulled up to A.C.'s terminal and spotted her at the curb, standing next to a duffel bag and a rolling suitcase.

"The flight alright?"

"I slept," she said, and laughed. "So, yeah, it was great."

Nigerians know how to dress. This is an undeniable fact.

But A.C. took that shit to the next level. Butch, and beautifully so. Her hair cut real low with a little line shaved into a side part. Fresh. She wore traditional Nigerian men's clothing—golden designs embroidered into a deep red agbada that came down to the middle of her calves. She wore a matching red sokoto underneath. She folded a large flowing sleeve over her right shoulder before lifting the duffel. I grabbed the suitcase and together we loaded her luggage into the trunk.

"It's so good to finally meet you!"

"Thank you for pickin me up." The bass in A.C.'s voice was unintentionally sultry—which made it all the more sultry.

I thought of Lee's reaction to me being here instead of at her game, and internally cringed.

"Bros, abeg! Of course!"

❦

Like old friends reunited, we took to each other. Our conversation flowed effortlessly as we cruised down the highway.

"My parents named me Agatha." She paused for optimum dramatic effect.

"Agatha fuckin Catherine Wọyintọnbra. I think they expected me to become a nun. I considered it. All those women and all that time alone with all those women? I *definitely* considered it."

I laughed at her off-handed blasphemy. Such a lovely reminder that blasphemy, like beauty, is definitely in the eye of the beholder.

"You'd have to convince them you was Jesus incarnate for them to get naked for you."

"Please. Nuns are the easiest to get with. I know my way around the Scripture and that's the only way to a nun's heart. That and, you know, a strong tongue."

I looked over at her in the passenger seat. "Na lie! You serious?"

"Taylor Ejiroghene, sisí èkó, yes, I swear o."

I laughed, then asked, "What ethnicity are you?"

"I'm Ijaw."

"Yes, Delta State ooo!"

"All day. Every. *Day.* You're Urhobo?"

"Yes, I am," I said. "You were in Naija recently right?"

"Yesyes! I was there for New Year's. It was beautiful, but there were times when I felt like a tourist in my own country and that broke my heart."

"What made you feel like a tourist?"

She sighed. "Well, I felt like I had to fit everything I wanted to do into a month, which was hard. Spending any time away from Naija, in the States and then returning, it's like people see you as American or Americanized just by virtue of the time you've been away."

"That's hard. Going home and having your own people see you as American is heartbreaking. For me, because I'd been away for several years, a lot of Nigerians—including my family—see me as oyibo … which is so strange to me since I see myself as Nigerian full stop."

"Exactly."

"When I'm in the States, I'm homesick and aching for my next expensive-ass, too-short trip home. I don't feel completely at home in the U.S. and I don't feel completely at home in Naija. And I'm always looking for how to be more Nigerian, more African, more informed about what's happening at home, and it's never enough."

"It never will be," A.C. said.

"Ever?"

"Ever. That's a fight you can't win so don't waste your time. In the 'who's this or that enough' contest, everyone loses."

I sighed, realizing she was probably right. "What's the queer scene like back home?"

"Secretive. But it exists. You just gotta have hella, *hella* tight gaydar." We laughed. "I actually usually only date African women and any exception is just that—an exception that proves the rule."

"Why is that?"

"We're fuckin beautiful. Period, full stop. That's my complete argument," A.C. said with unabashed pride. "It took some time, but I've found my community of first-generation and immigrant African dykes in the Bay. Who would have thought that I'd find that in Cali? We make each other feel at home and I think it's with them that I feel closest to myself. Does that makes sense?"

"Definitely makes sense," I said. "I'm sure being with an African woman means they understand so much of what non-Africans don't. Sometimes I get tired of explaining shit that's so basic to me."

"Like …?"

"Like how to pronounce my name and 'no I am *not* Yorùbá or Igbo or whatever you read about in your Intro to Black Studies class.' I love my Yorùbá, Hausa and Igbo folks, but there's hundreds of other ethnicities in Naija besides those three."

"Exactly! Assuming I'm Yorùbá because I'm Nigerian is like assuming every Latina I meet is Mexican or Puerto Rican," A.C. said.

"Meanwhile, homegirl could be from Ecuador or—"

"—Colombia or Panama. I feel you, you *know* I feel you," she said. "I majored in African Studies. In some ways it was so liberating to learn about Africa in an academic setting and to read the opinions of African scholars. In other ways, it was the most over-generalized study of Swahili, Zulu and Yorùbá culture and people. I created an individualized minor in Nigerian Delta Studies, which was dope."

"Wow … That sounds sooo amazing! The Delta Studies part, not the over-generalized African Studies part. Even the concept of 'African Studies' is so fuckin general. In the Africana Studies courses I've taken, people look at me like they want an expert opinion on the assigned reading. It gets on my nerves."

"It's polar opposites for me," A.C. said. "Either people ignore that I'm Nigerian, or they put me on the spot about it every chance they get, asking me random questions about Naija geography or history."

I parked in front of her hotel. "You should ask them about U.S. geography," I said, smiling. "Ask them about the mountains of Nevada and ask for specific latitude and longitude coordinates to go camping." She laughed, and I continued. "It's so funny that immigrants get treated so poorly in this country. The ones that go for citizenship probably know more about U.S. history than folks born and raised here. How many of your U.S.-born friends do you think know who fuckin wrote 'The Star Spangled Banner'?"

We laughed as we hopped out of the car.

A.C.'s performance the following night was powerfully moving and unlike anything I'd ever experienced before. She incorporated poetry with the Socratic method and had an improvisational question-and-answer session with the audience. She started her performance like a conversation:

"What it do?"

Silence.

"Oh, I forgot for a second that I'm in New York. How you feelin?" There were murmurs. She reached up and grabbed her earlobe. "I no dey hear you o. *How you feelin?*" The crowd in the auditorium responded loudly with a medley of "Ai'ight" and "Good."

A.C. wore a turquoise and yellow sokoto with a matching loose-fitting, short-sleeved buba that stopped mid-thigh. Around her neck were thick, dark coral beads that reminded me of the Delta. She was barefoot.

"Show of hands, how many people in here have a body?"

Everyone's hands went up.

"Keep your hands up. Now, how many folks in here have a gender identity?"

Some hands went down.

"Some of you put your hands down. Funny thing is we *all* have a gender identity. Even if your identity is that you *think* you don't have one."

She walked back and forth across the stage.

"Gender is a funny thing. People want you to stay in your little box so they feel good about theirs. We all think our gender is original. We're all right … and we're all wrong." A.C. smiled. "So much of what we think is just our natural way of doing things—for example, how we hold our bodies, our gestures, how we walk—is all learned behavior. We *learn* how to be ourselves partly from our own instincts, yes, and also from what we see around us—on television, in magazines, in music videos, in school, at home."

"Some folks," she said, "when they see someone who is

making up who they are from somewhere *other* than media and our oppressive societal status quo, it bothers them so much … I think mostly because no one told them that they, too, *can do whatever the fuck they want with their bodies and gender.* So they hate hard. They hate that they didn't know they could be a gender-bending shero. They hate the repressed desire in their own body to bust out of the gender box that imprisons them. You could call this shit homophobia, heterosexism, transphobia. To me, it boils down to 'damn I ain't know I could do that, so why should you be able to?'"

She touched on many topics in her performance, weaving through it all a theme of self-expression as an exercise of liberation from gender constructs and stereotypes of ethnicity and race.

"Your eyes crowded with a million memories you don't share with me, and I know you got questions for me," A.C. said, smiling. She encouraged feedback from the audience and asked questions of her own. The whole show transformed into a massive conversation between several hundred people.

It was magical.

☙❧

A.C. and I embraced when I dropped her off at the airport the next morning.

She felt like home.

"Hit me up anytime, Oghene. Naija dykes need to take care of each other, abi?"

"Abi," I said, and smiled.

☙❧

After dropping A.C. off at JFK, I drove to Lee's apartment. I considered going upstairs ... and then ... I just didn't.

I don't want to fight, I thought as put the car into park in front of her apartment building. Shaking my head, I shoved the guilt I still felt for missing her game to the perimeters of my consciousness. I dropped her car keys in her mailbox and took the train home.

FOR SIZAKELE

bittersweet passion

"Quelle heure est-il?" Sy murmured to herself. She checked the time on her phone, then stuffed her gloved hands into her pockets and tried to quell the slight fluttering in her belly. She found herself attempting to swallow the irresistible smiles that crept up as she waited for Taylor on the corner of Astor Place and Lafayette. Sy pulled her hoodie onto her head. Then swiped it off her head. She was first-date-nervous for dinner with a friend. A friend. An acquaintance, really. Not a date. So totally *not* a date.

Sy spotted Taylor walking across the street toward her. Sy's heartbeat sped up as she looked Taylor up and down, admiring her style. Taylor wore skinny jeans, a mid-thigh-length winter coat that hugged her curvy figure and a crocheted scarf, which was draped over her head, framing her beautiful face.

"Bonjour. How bodi?" Sy asked.

"I dey kampke," Taylor said, and smiled.

"I thought maybe I wasn't gonna get to see you ever again," Sy said.

"Why?"

"Because you're such a busy, busy diva." Taylor laughed. "By the way, the show was amazing. You did such a good job organizing it."

"Thank you!" Sy hid a smile as she watched Taylor glow with pride. "Thank you for coming. I'm sorry I didn't get to talk to you after the show; things got a little hectic."

"Pas de problème; it's all good."

"I'm *so* happy everything went as planned." Taylor sighed with relief. "For a little while there, I was nervous about how it was gonna go. You hungry?"

"Oui."

"Where do you want to eat?" Taylor asked.

"It doesn't matter to me. Are you craving anything in particular?"

"I *really* want some Nigerian food."

Sy thought for a moment. "Well, I know there's a Nigerian restaurant called Banga. It's uptown on Malcolm X."

"Alright. You wanna take the bus up? We can talk and enjoy the city above ground."

"You don't enjoy the lovely aroma of our subway system?" Sy teased.

"I know you're playing, so I won't even answer that!"

The bus uptown showed them a bisection of the city as one neighborhood morphed into the next. From the Village to Chelsea to Herald Square to Times Square, Midtown, the Upper West Side, past Columbia and deeper into Harlem. Brooklyn was the heart of New York and Harlem was its spine, holding the city in place. Something about Harlem's Blackness screamed *home* to Sy. They got off the bus at 125th Street. Smoke billowed out of a small bowl that sat on a street vendor's table. The intoxicating smell of burning amber filled Sy's lungs and soothed her.

The restaurant was on the second floor of a building nestled between an African imports shop and an African hair-braiding salon. They were seated and handed menus. Their table overlooked Malcolm X Boulevard, a street lined with vendors selling oils, incense, cell phone cases, purses, jewelry, shea butter and soap. Pedestrians bustled by and music blasted just out of earshot, serving as a distant soundtrack to their evening.

After ordering their food, Sy asked, "So what's your wife like?"

"If I'm married, someone should have told me. My *girlfriend* is beautiful, sweet—a basketball-playin pianist. Not many people know about her love affair with the piano." Taylor smiled proudly, then abruptly asked, "Are you seeing anyone?"

Sy wondered why she cared to know, since her girlfriend sounded pretty amazing. Sy averted her eyes and answered a simple "No."

"That wasn't a very convincing 'no'."

Sy laughed. "I know." She sighed and thought of Elle. "Is there always an ex that lingers, literally or emotionally?"

"Unfortunately, for most of us, yes. Is the lingering bittersweet for you?"

Sy rolled her eyes.

"Okay … So more bitter than sweet?"

Sy sighed again, remembering the warmth of Elle's luscious thickness in her arms.

Their food arrived, pausing their conversation. Sy watched Taylor's face as she savored the spicy flavors of her moin moin.

Taylor resumed her questioning. "Alrighty then, I guess it's just bitter?"

Sy laughed loudly. "I don't know anymore, how can you stay sweet about a bitter situation?"

"I do *not* fuckin know. I'm good at holding a grudge, so I'm not the one to be asking."

"I love the food here," Sy said, diving into her jollof rice.

"It's not as good as my mama's, but it's very good. You're changing the subject."

"Yes ma'am. Hopefully you'll let me."

"Okay," Taylor said. "I keep forgetting to ask you for the Copy Cat account number so I can have the funds for the copies transferred—"

"Don't worry about it."

"But—"

"Forget it."

"It has to be paid for," Taylor insisted.

"Not really. It's not like anyone but us knows those copies were made."

"What if you get in trouble?"

"I won't." Sy smiled. "Stop protesting and accept that you got the hookup."

"Ai'ight … but I'm definitely treating you to dinner."

"You will get no protest from me on that."

She has a girlfriend, she has a girlfriend was Sy's internal mantra for the rest of the night. Taylor was cute. The way she averted her eyes after Sy deliberately embraced her a few seconds longer than normal. How Taylor's smile lit up her face—especially her eyes. Taylor was adorable. Their evening was fun. More fun than it was safe to be having with someone with a girlfriend.

held

There was a rapid succession of hard knocks on my dorm room door. I had only been in my room for a minute, and barely had my jacket off. Startled, I looked through the peephole, then opened the door, puzzled. "What—?"

"Where were you, Taylor?"

"Calm down, baby," I said. I closed the door behind her.

"I'm calm. I just wondered where you were since you must have lost my number. I've been calling you all day." Lee peeled off her coat and threw it on the chair in the corner.

"What? Were you waiting here for me to come home?"

"Yes," Lee said, flatly. "I know you don't have class today, so where were you?"

I sat down on my bed. "I was out."

"Out where?"

"Out—side," I said, smiling. "Out—of the closet…"

"Be serious! Where were you?"

"I went out to an early dinner. I turned my phone off; that's why I didn't get any of your calls."

"You had time for dinner but didn't have time to come to my fuckin game?"

"That's not fair—"

She put her hand up to halt my speech. "Whatever. Who the fuck did you have dinner with?"

"A friend."

"A male friend?"

"No. Why would you assume that?"

"Because you like them so damn much."

I leaned back on my elbows. "Now that you mention it, Ahsha, me and two dudes we picked up at the pool hall up the street got a hotel room and had the best fourgy ever. I didn't know that girl was so flexible—*wow.*" I rolled my eyes. "I don't know why you always tryin to hold the fact that I like men over my head."

"I don't know what you see in them."

"It's called *orientation*. You don't have to understand it."

She stormed toward me and stopped. "I see you looking at the dudes on the corner."

"Because they look *good,*" I said unapologetically, leaning forward. "Like you don't be checking out the lipstick femmes. *Please.*"

"But they're women."

"So? They're not me and that's the point. Besides, you've fucked more men than me. I've actually never fucked a man. *By the way.* Just a little reminder of that fun fact." *I know I can't quantify dykeness. I'm not "more of a dyke" because I've slept with fewer men than her. But my point got made.*

"But I could never marry one or …"

"Like that matters? You married your pussy to his dick, what's the difference whether or not you stay with him?"

"You could actually spend the rest of your life with a man."

"Yeah, if he was a fierce feminist and made me happy, sure. You tight? Am I supposed to apologize for that?"

She shrugged. "I guess not, since you're probably gonna end up with a man."

"What scientific method of analysis did you use to come up with that *flawed* hypothesis?" I asked.

"It's obvious."

I stood up, facing her. "How is it obvious, Lee?"

"It just is."

"Well, where does that leave you and me if I'm supposed to end up with a man?"

She shrugged. "You'll probably leave me for a man," she said, so matter-of-factly I thought I must've heard wrong. I involuntarily stepped back from the impact of her words.

"I'm gonna *what?*"

"It's true. Bisexual women always leave their butches for

men."

"Do you think I'm just kickin it with you to pass time until my Mandingo warrior in shining armor comes and saves me?" I sucked my teeth. "Is that *really* what you think about me? That I'm gonna leave you any minute?"

"Not any minute …" she said. "Just ... eventually."

"What is it about dick that you think is so hypnotic, so powerful that it could pull me away from the only person I've ever loved?"

"Because it's easier to be with a man than it is to be with a woman. It's easier to just be straight like everybody else."

I stepped forward. "Lee, it would be harder for me to pretend to be someone I'm not. What makes being a dyke even harder is being told by my woman that I'm gonna leave her. Did you ever think that maybe why *some* bi women *may* leave their butches for men is because their butches push them away with statements like the one you just made?" I didn't give her a chance to respond. "Or maybe some of these hardcore 'lesbians' are really bi and just know no one will feel them if they come out as bi in their dyke community. And let's be real, Lee, you've been with more men than me. Chances are greater that you'll leave me for one than the other way around."

Lee turned away, clenching and unclenching her fists at her sides. "That's bullshit, Taylor. That's fuckin ridiculous."

"Is it?"

"Yes."

"Why is it ridiculous to think that you could fuck a man again and like it enough to stay with him?"

"That was my past!" she yelled, turning back to face me.

"So?"

"I'm fuckin telling you I'm not into dudes anymore."

"Oh … you mean like I *fuckin told you* that I'm not gonna cheat on you with a man? Like that?" I sighed, then abruptly said, "You know what? I'm tired of this damn conversation. I have this same conversation with so many butch dykes. It's like our roles were picked for us. It's old."

"So what are you sayin?"

I was suddenly weary. "Can we talk about it later?" I walked closer and stood in front of her, willing my anger out of my body as I lifted my fingers to her lips. "Kiss me."

"Why don't you kiss *me?*" There was insecure resentment in her voice. I tried not to roll my eyes. And kissed her. Her tongue hesitantly entered my mouth, then became hot and passionate. I moved my chest closer to hers as her hand tightened at the back of my waist; I whispered a moan, my hands cupping her face. She roughly pushed me toward the bed with her body, shocking me. I stopped kissing her for a second, confused. *Was she still … mad—?*

She slipped her tongue in my ear, but I felt eerily detached from her touch. Coldly, I asked, "Like it?"

"Huh?" she mumbled.

"Do you like it?" I asked again, expecting her to hear the distance in my voice.

"Of course I do," she mumbled. We fell onto the bed. The sudden weight of her body took my breath away. I could feel her hard thighs between mine, forcing them wider. I tried to wiggle free but her weight locked me in place. *Damn she's strong.* I half-laughed, nervous. " Ai'ight Lee, get off me."

She laughed loudly in my ear, then grabbed my wrists and pinned them to the bed above my head. I clenched my fists under her grip. "What're you doin?" My heart fluttered ...

… with fear? Whateva. Chill, Taylor, chill.

"Nothin we ain't done before," she whispered. *What the fuck—?* Her tone scared me. She moved my wrists together, pinning them with one hand; her free hand reached under my sweater and grabbed my breast with a harshness that hurt. "Lee—!" She clasped her mouth over mine before I could finish. She pushed her tongue into my mouth, flicking over my teeth and tongue. Was this the same tongue that had made love to me? It couldn't be. I shook my head to clear my mind and loosen her mouth's grip on mine. *It couldn't be.*

"Who the fuck were you with?" she growled.

"S-Sy."

"Who the fuck is that?"

"A friend."

Lee kissed me again. "Gehoffme—" The rest of my words were muffled by her mouth. I strained against her hands as her grip around my wrists grew tighter. Never before had I been more aware of the power contained within her body than now as it was held over and against me. I turned my head violently away from her kiss. She moved her lips down my neck.

"Stop it—" She pulled my sweater and bra up with her free hand and sucked on my breast. "Lee, I'm not playin with you." Her tongue and lips were hot and wet on my body. My body felt lost to me, no longer mine.

Hers.

"Don't front like—" she said.

Her hands/reached for my belt buckle/undid it/unsnapped jeans.

"Lee, get the fuck up off me!"

"We've done this before," she said, tightening her grip around my wrists again.

Her fingers/firm at the top of my panties/pressed into my pelvic bone/pulled my pants down.

"You're wet," she said.

"No, I'm not!"

She touched my clit through my panties. "You will be."

"Don't."

"Don't … what? Don't touch?" She grabbed my hips harshly. "Did you fuck her?"

"What?"

Her hand jumped from between my legs to around my neck. "Did. You. Fuck. Her!"

I was terrified. "N-no!"

"I don't believe you." She tightened her hand around my

throat.

"I didn't!"

"Say it again!"

"I didn't touch her!" Lee's grip got tighter. I was having a hard time breathing.

"Say it again."

"I—" trying to draw in air "—didn't fuck her." My throat felt like it was collapsing into itself.

My breath quickened; my heartbeat was an erratic freight train. Tears rolled down my face into my ears.

She came closer to me to kiss me and I bit her lip. Hard. Her body jerked off of mine. I rolled off the bed so quickly I fell to the floor. Gasping for air and coughing, I struggled to put the length of the room between us.

"We've done this before!"

"No! We have *never* done that ever. Never fuckin ever!"

"Whateva," she said, and turned her back to me.

"Whatever *what?*" I snapped, knowing the only power I had over her was the jagged broken edges around my words.

"The stupid games you play," she muttered.

Speechless and disgusted, I glared at the Berlin Wall of her back.

"How is me saying no and you ignoring that a game? Is that how you prove how much you can control me?" I struggled to regulate my breathing. "I thought we were supposed to be better than straight people, but here we go, doin the same fucked up shit."

"What the fuck does that mean?"

"You, the 'butch,' holding me, the 'femme,' down. Too predictable. You were actin like a sexist man."

"Don't call me a man just because you can't handle the fact that I don't wear dresses or heels or makeup. I'm still a woman, Taylor."

"Noooo. You got a pussy but with a dick brain. I never cared about the clothes you wear, you *know* that. This isn't even about that. What the hell happened to consent?"

"You liked it!"

"No, I didn't!"

"Yes—"

"How are you gonna tell me what the fuck I liked!" All my rage at being a powerless little femme at her mercy boiled up and overflowed like a waterfall in a teacup. "Who gave you the muthafuckin right to hold me down? Do you even *realize* how fucked up that was?"

"Don't scream at me," she said, suddenly quiet.

"Or what? Or you'll tie me up and beat me?"

Tears careened
uncontrolled
down the curves
of my cheekbones.

"Could you chill out, Taylor?" She sighed, speaking softly to the floor, her head in her hands. "You're giving me a damn headache." Lee was eerily calm, as she always was whenever she was really mad.

"Don't tell *me* to chill out." I paced around, up and down the room. "I can't believe this shit. Don't you understand what just happened? *I. Said. Stop.*"

"You're actin like we've never done this before."

"Have I ever said 'stop' before?"

Silence.

"Ever ever *ever,* Lee?"

"I—"

"You what?" I was standing in front of her. I moved until I was between her legs, my thighs pressing against the top of her bent head. "You what?" I asked again, raising my voice.

"Back up, Taylor."

"I thought you liked being close to me. What? Am I making you uncomfortable?"

She raised her head. "Why are you being such a bitch?"

"You don't own my body just because I let you fuck me,

Lee. What? You tryin to add 'rapist' to your resume?"

"Shut the fuck up!" Lee stood up and glared down at me. "Why are you tryin to start some shit?"

"I'm not starting shit, Lee, *you* started this—or did you forget already about what just went down?"

"You always blowing shit—"

"—out of proportion. Yeah, whatever, *bitch*."

She froze. "What'd you call me?"

"You heard me."

She pointed at me with her index finger. "Chris, don't you *ever*—"

I slapped her hand away. "Get your fingers out my damn face." Heartbeat. "Did you just call me Chris?"

She raised her hand again and I slapped it away, again. Harder this time.

"Don't hit me," she said.

"Chris, your cousin? Chris … who raped you? Why the fuck would you call me his name?"

She grabbed my shoulder roughly and glared at me like she hated me. I stared back defiantly, trying to look fearless. I shook my shoulder out from under her grip and pushed against her chest.

Lee pushed past me, grabbed her coat from the chair, and threw "Fuck you, Taylor" over her shoulder.

The violent slam of the door made me flinch, but I was glad she was gone, glad to be alone, glad to be a little free.

Free ... to breathe. I rushed to the door and locked it behind her, anxious to have control over something. *Who the fuck does she think she is?* She'd held me down like I was her property and she could do whatever she wanted to me. I thought loving women was supposed to be easier. If I wanted to deal with misogynist, sexist shit I'd fuck a man, not her.

I'm not gonna cry. I'm gonna stay calm. I breathed in, filling my chest with air. *She must hate me … she must really hate me.* I walked to my window and drew the curtains closed, darkening my room. Dark, thick thoughts ran all over my room, crashing against walls, chairs, my closet, stumbling over my shoes, and then raced back into me through nostrils, ears, skin.

Can't hide from your own thoughts, girl.

But why not? Why can't I postpone the pain? Just ignore it like my credit card bills?

My phone rang. I didn't know who it was, but I knew who it wasn't.

"Hello?" My voice was monotone.

"Hey, it's Sy. I'm just calling to make sure you got home safe."

"I'm fine. Can I call you back?"

"Sure," she said. "Are you okay?"

"Uh-huh," I lied. "Call you later."

I hung up.

Fuck! What did I do to deserve this *shit?* I sat at the head of my bed, leaned against my pillows, and watched my hands fold and unfold in my lap. Folding and unfolding to distract my mind from the hot tears burning a path down my cheeks.

"No Lee—fuck *you*."

ଔଓ

It hurt so bad I curled into a ball and pretended I was inside my mama. I bit my lip hard, trying to distract myself from the pain grating at my heart piece by section by bit by fragment by part.

Her grip around my wrists grew tighter. "Get the fuck up off me!" I turned my head violently away from her kiss. "Stop it—" My heart fluttered with fear … I clenched my fists. "You liked it." "We've done this before." "Have I ever said 'stop' before?"

Looking at me like she hated me, hated me, hates *me.*

"Fuck you, Taylor."

Never had I been more thankful to live alone than at that moment. I lay on my side, knees pressed against my chest, hands gripping my face, crying so hard my body shook.

Is this love?

I said stop. And she didn't.

I didn't care who heard me cry. Time must have passed because light no longer leaked into the room through the edges of my curtain. The unexpected ringing of my phone frightened me into an upright position. *Why is it so loud?* I snatched it up.

"Hello?"

"Taylor, it's Sy again." She sounded apologetic.

I said nothing.

"Taylor?"

"Yes?" I answered numbly.

"Is everything alright?"

"No."

"Do you want me to come over?"

"It doesn't matter, but I'm getting off the phone now."

"Tay—"

I hung up.

I went over to my stereo, put in Meshell Ndegeocello's *Comfort Woman* CD and pressed repeat. I turned the volume and bass up as loud as it could go, letting the speakers thump. *I dare any of my loud-ass neighbors to call and tell me to turn my shit down.*

Meshell's voice was everywhere, making my room seem full, though the only thing it was truly full of was the emptiness inside me. I sank to the floor, sitting with my legs pulled up to my chest, holding myself like I was the last valuable thing I had left, because I was.

ᏋᏋ

The knocks at my door turned into pounding, and even then I barely heard it over Meshell's voice. I turned the music down on my way to the door, looked through the peephole and saw Sy standing there. I slowly opened the door. I was in an altered state of mind; I was not the same woman she'd met a couple weeks ago, not the same woman she'd had dinner with earlier. I knew I would not be able to find the energy to be that woman for her now. *This girl will have to do.*

Dammit, I am so tired.

"Taylor—"

"Shhh," I whispered. Taking her hand in mine, I pulled her into my room and immediately locked the door, suddenly scared Lee would burst in. I led her to the side of my bed.

"Take off your coat and shoes."

She did.

Her eyes looked worried. She gently cupped the side of my face with a palm that felt like satin feathers and asked: "Chérie, qu'est-ce qui s'est passé? "

I could only shake my head, wet eyes looking at her feet.

"Rien," I said. "Je sais nous sont les étrangers, mais … can you come lay with me?"

We lay on top of my comforter facing each other. I snuggled into her warm body and sighed.

I sighed … and sighed … and sighed until my chest shook, making my breathing jagged. Sy's arms tightened around me, stroking my neck, holding my body safe. "Come here, baby," she whispered, drawing me closer. My head nestled into her neck, and I let the lava of my tears flow. Our legs tangled; my palms grasped her back. We were belly to belly and our breathing was in sync.

"She makes me want to hate her," I said coldly.

"Your girlfriend?"

I nodded.

"What'd she do?"

"She held me down when I said no," I said, the words piercing me as I spoke them. She put a soothing hand on my shoulder.

"Mon Dieu! Qu'est-ce qui s'est passé?"

"She was mad we went out to eat. She kept asking me if we fucked. She wouldn't believe me when I said no. I told her to stop and she wouldn't. When she finally got off me, I called her a bitch, which made her really mad, and then I thought she was gonna hit me." I stopped, thinking it would have been better if she *had* hit me, because then I would've had an excuse to hit her back. "Maybe she'll hit me next time."

Sy pulled me to her and placed a delicate kiss on my forehead. "I hate her," I said. "She choked me! Lee has never grabbed me with that much roughness, *ever* … She's so much fuckin stronger than me. I couldn't even get up from under her! No matter how hard I tried, I couldn't. I just couldn't. *Fuck.*" I clenched and unclenched my fists. "I hate her for that."

"Chérie—"

"I really do! And on top of all that she thinks I'm a straight woman stuck in a bisexual girl's body playing dyke for the semester until I get over my little phase, curiosity, or whatever the *fuck* she thinks I'm going through. I always have to prove my fuckin authenticity to her." I pulled away. "I can't be near you. I'm so full of anger right now." *I want to hit Lee, that's what I* really *want. I want to hurt her back, make her feel like she can't do anything but beg me for muthafuckin mercy. Bitch.*

Fuck you, Taylor. Her voice played over and over in my head.

Agitated, I swung my legs over the side of the bed, sitting where Lee had sat not too long ago. My hands gripped and ungripped the side of the bed; I slowly rocked back and forth.

"I do everything for her. I give her so much of myself," I said. I stared into my lap. "Sometimes, I don't know if there's anything left for me."

"Is it okay if I hold you?" Sy asked in the most tender voice.

"Yes."

From behind, Sy slipped one arm like honey over my shoulder and across my chest, then the other around my waist, pulling me firmly back into her. "Come here." My body tensed slightly, not knowing how to be, not knowing if I could trust her. "Lean back," she whispered into my ear.

"I don't know how," I mumbled.

"It's okay, let me take care of you."

… take care of you … take care of you … take care of you …

Sy's words dripped like raindrops onto the thirsty sand of my bruised heart. I could feel her kindness melting me. Her tenderness was strong enough to prevent me from putting up any barriers. She cupped my body in hers. A weight I didn't know was there was lifted off me.

Sy was strong for me, stroking my hair and shoulders. I didn't feel like I had to hold everything up, prove anything or be anybody in particular. I was *so fuckin tired* … and hurt and sad, feeling disillusioned and powerless and lonely.

And shaking with an anger that scared the shit out of me.

FOR SIZAKELE

"WHY WON'T YOU LET ME DANCE?"

she demands of me from the inside of the mirror.
she is flat, one-dimensional, paper-thin/
unable to manifest because she is stuck within
my disbelief in our ability.

she is stuck on the inside of that mirror
immobilized
by my wish to make untruths true like:
we can't dance.

on her side of the mirror, she is: frustrated, hands
on round hips,
hitting tips of toes
impatiently against wooden floor.

unbeknownst to me
she watches me across the gigantic psychic space
between us/
she watches me looking into the looking glass,
looking into her blankly/
looking unseeingly through her,
hypnotized by my own lack of vision.
she snaps her fingers in my face. *"Yo!"*

she moves across the glass as I stand still,
hoping maybe *then* I'll notice her
But I'm not
looking anymore.

sweat has made our brown body glisten.
she gazes at me lovingly
hoping I'll trust her enough to let her womanifest
inside our body—
I wear a gray sports bra under a loose, off-shoulder shirt
baggy gray pants—
typical dancer clothes,
she smiles.

Sunlight shines
through the twin bay windows onto my back,
gleaming into her eyes.

Making a wide-based, upside-down "V" with my legs,
I fold my torso delicately over them.
Maybe I'm not flexible enough
I say into the empty studio,
swinging my torso to my right leg and hanging over it,
Guess I'm not experienced enough—oh, I'm sorry.
I shake my head, confused.
Shit—
I let my torso hang down the middle of my legs.
"Are you scared of what we can do?" she asks me
Maybe I'm just not good enough I say.
I can't hear her because
my spiritual ear plugs are in.
Whispering as I stand upright and spin in place:

if I could describe to you
what's inside of me,
maybe then you could call me a poet—
wrap up my people,
send us to amerikkka
then watch time unfold it.

FOR SIZAKELE

No, I can't dance I say angrily as I drop abruptly
to the floor.
Flat on my back, I place my hands on the floor
above my head,
raise my whole body up, making a bridge with my body;
I lower myself back to the floor,
slip down onto the side of my left thigh,
planting my palm firmly on the floor,
running in a circle around my palm, chasing myself/
maybe
running away from her.
I slide smooth like spilling water,
[if only I could see myself … she thinks to ourself]
I glide sensually …
Rolling onto my back, I curl my body up into itself,
and do a back spin.
And no,
I'm not a dancer!

She whispers to me:

"But I *want to dance*
I *am a dancer*
and I *dance.*
… look at me, baby."

I looked into her eyes for the first time since I was 7.

Love? I murmur,
hesitant heart open.

"Yes?" she answers.

Silence.

Then:

Love ... please ...
teach me how to dance.

FOR SIZAKELE

tastes like home

Stepping out of the Dance Building was like moving from one world into another.

I hesitated on the brink, gazing across the space between the two … lingering just inside of Dance. I felt my worlds spinning at different speeds on almost perpendicular axes. In the deepest parts of me, I wanted dance to be part of my everyday instead of something I had to squeeze in between everything else.

My eyes caressed the space between my worlds and I was at ease for the first time since I'd cried in Sy's arms. I almost didn't care that I hadn't spoken to Lee in three days, that I had slept through all of my classes today and that, even after 15 hours of sleep, I was still, inexplicably, sleepy.

Am I depressed? Yeah, I think I'm officially depressed.

My limbs were loose, as if every muscle had been perfectly stretched by a loving masseuse. I slowly rolled my shoulders up and back, exhaled and floated down the front steps.

Snow tumbled down like tiny feathers floating in slow motion, leaving a light dusting of white on the sidewalk.

People rushed down the sidewalk every which way, most of them students; some were pre-occupied as they walked aimlessly chatting on phones, some looked frazzled, others looked like they had their lives handled. Broadway's traffic was aggressive and belied the peace I'd felt within Dance.

Brisk, cold air moved swiftly, as if in a hurry. Someone whistled. I turned toward the sound, and saw Sy strolling over.

"Hey, sexy mama," she said, and smiled. Sy wore a bright headwrap that formed a bun at the nape of her neck; it was topped by a black fedora, cocked to the side. A short black peacoat, jeans and flat, calf-length boots completed her look.

I smiled, pleased to see her. "What's up?"

"Nothin," she said, her dimples digging into her cheeks. She playfully pinched my bare tummy beneath my off-shoulder shirt. "Where you goin? Why is your coat hangin open like it's not brick out here?"

"I don't even know," I said absently.

Sy zipped up my coat, and lightly placed a hand on my waist. Snowflakes rested on her long eyelashes. She asked, "How've you been?"

I forced a half-smile. "I'm fine." Sy gave me a *don't-give-me-that-bullshit* look.

"What?"

She sighed and shook her head. "You hungry?"

"I'm always hungry."

"Then come home with me and let me cook for you."

"What you makin?"

"Nothin much … just some fufu—"

"Excuse me!" I grabbed her arm, suddenly excited. I hadn't had fufu since the last time I visited my mama. "Where did you get fufu?"

"Brooklyn, USA, where else?"

I laughed. "Girl … What kind of soup are you making with it?"

"Egusi."

"Oh my *Goddess!*" I screamed, not caring who heard. "Your people make egusi soup too?"

"Yes, and yours do too, right?"

"Yes."

"Well, then I want to make it for you … if that's okay?" She seemed suddenly unsure. I wanted to cry at her sweet humility. She looked apprehensive, scared I might be offended. I wrapped my arms around her, hugging her tightly. I was thankful for her kindness and tried to transmit that gratitude to her.

"Of course it's okay, Sy."

Fufu glided down my throat.

The poet has no words.

Tastes like home.

With the exception of restaurants, no one outside of my family had ever cooked Nigerian food for me. My heart fluttered a bit. *I feel at home with her.* I didn't have to explain my culture, my dykehood or my femmeness to Sy, I could just *be.* That felt like a new kind of free I hadn't known I needed.

"My belle full, thank you. And thank you for being—" the words stumbled, then tumbled out of me "—there for me the other day, you really—"

"Please, whatever, you don't have to thank me."

"Yes, I do. I really, really do." My eyes met hers, and though I was calm from Dance, I was hurt from Lee, and it showed. The pain in my eyes was too vivid to hide. I looked down at my soup, studied its orange with flecks of green bitter leaf, chunks of beef and dried fish. "Thank you. I felt like I was unraveling ... or something. You're very sweet." I gazed out the window beside Sy's dinner table; it overlooked neighboring apartment buildings, grocery stores and local businesses. Endless buildings in every direction stood defiant against the late afternoon sky.

"I just wanted to try to make you feel a little better."

"You did. You keep saving me, first with the copies, then with the other day." It had felt good in her arms. *It had felt so good in her arms.*

"It's cool, whatever I can do." She smiled, then got a little more serious. "How is everything?"

"I'm gonna wash my hands before this fufu gets hard." I got up, went to the kitchen and washed my hands under warm water. *Why hasn't Lee called me? Why haven't I called her? Why am I so apathetic about the whole fuckin thing?*

Sy came over and washed her hands beside me. "We don't have to talk about it if you don't want to."

Loud ass, bold ass, poe poe slammin diva, but words shrink and hide when asked to describe...

My voice got small. "I—I'm sorry if I seem … weird. I can't find words to explain anything."

"Don't apologize. You *really* don't have to explain anything to me, Taylor."

ଔ෴ଓ

We spent the rest of the day talking, and the night watching Nollywood films.

Then we made fun of Nollywood films.

"Dis one here o—*ah ah.*" I pointed at her television. "Wetin kind woman go chase man with no naira, no job, no *motivation,*" I said.

"*Eh heh.* Na her own choice, sef. We no know wetin kind love she dey feel."

"Abeg! She go chop love? Love go pay am rent? By fire or by force, I go make you hear word tonight." I sucked my teeth.

"Odaro, you no dey scare me o," Sy warned, laughing. "You no get *sense.*"

"I no get sense?" I feigned anger. "*I* no get sense?" I spoke to an imaginary audience. "The audacity of dis one oooo." I looked back at her. "Am I your mate?"

"Abeg, I senior you now."

"By what? Five minutes?"

"One year. Respect your elders, ojare," she said. I burst out laughing. "I love Nollywood. You know Nigeria has the second largest film industry in the world?"

"Is that all?" I said. "I'm surprised it's not number one."

It had been dark for a while when we got tired. She offered to walk me to the train, and when I asked, "Who's gonna walk back with you?" she said, "Me."

"I don't want you walking home alone at this time of night," I said.

"I walk alone at night all the time," she said.

"Okay, but I don't feel right letting you walk home alone

at—" I glanced at her wall clock "—2 a.m. Especially if you're walking *me* to the train so *I* can get home safe."

"I'll be okay," she reassured me. I gave her a look that said, *hell no.* "Well, then, you might as well sleep over—as long as you're okay with that."

I asked for extra blankets, assuming I would take the couch. Sy laughed, and insisted I share her bed. She gave me a pair of boxers and a loose shirt to wear, as well as a towel and washcloth. "There's all kinds of smell-goods in the bathroom; feel free to use any and all of them."

Her bathroom was the sexiest, most elegant room I had ever seen. When I flipped the light switch, the room was flooded with a relaxing burnt orange glow; the floor tiles were a spotless, glossy red that matched the dried rose petals sprinkled on the back of the toilet and by the faucets of the sink. Except for the red rose petals and tile, everything else was white. I took the hottest, most luxurious shower, and my nostrils filled with the sweet coconut smell of her face and body washes. I dried off with a plush, mango-orange towel and languidly rubbed vanilla-scented lotion into my skin. Before leaving her bathroom spa, I wiggled my toes into her bathroom mat one last time; it felt like a bed of feathers.

I walked into Sy's bedroom. "I had *the* most amazing shower of my life. If I had that bathroom I would never comot for dis house," I said. "Is this place really expensive?"

"No, I'm blessed. My auntie let me move in under her lease when she moved to Harlem a few years ago. Since she'd been in this apartment for fifteen years, it was and still is rent-controlled."

"That's amazing. You know you can't ever let this apartment go, right?"

Sy laughed. "Exactly."

The walls of her bedroom were covered with huge poster-sized photographs of what I assumed was a Cameroonian village. I could see candor spilling from the faces; hear loud laughter from lips and feel passion pulsing from within the frames. Each image was alive with the love of the photographer. They were *spectacular* works of art.

"You took these photographs, right?"

"Yes."

"They're *amazing.*"

"Thank you."

"In Cameroon?"

"Yeah, in my grandmother's village. I took them the last time I was home." Her voice was warm and full of love. "I miss home, you know?"

I sighed heavily. "Yes, girl, I definitely know."

She pointed to her right. "On that wall is my 1884 series, the one I was telling you about."

My gaze followed her finger. I saw a cluster of about ten 11-by-17-inch photographs depicting various scenes: a busy African city with gigantic liquor and cigarette billboards jutting awkwardly against the beautiful trees they hung over. Teenagers with Tupac Shakur shirts, rockin jeans and sneakers. Plastic and garbage cluttered on the sides of the go-slow. A crisp, new Bible turned to the 23rd Psalm, laying on a well-worn wooden pulpit. A close-up of a pamphlet about the curses to befall one who did not accept Jesus Christ as their Lord and Savior. A baby being baptized; holy water droplets hanging in mid-air above the baby's forehead. My favorite was the photo of a group of men engaged in a lively conversation; the focal point was the cigarette in the hand of a man making a passionate point, the smoke unfurling upward as he gestured.

The liquor store billboards in Cameroon reminded me of the liquor stores on every other Brooklyn corner. Colonization through intoxication.

"Madiko," I said, melody in my voice like an afrobeat song. "Your work is phenomenal."

"Merci, merci."

Sy had the most extensive collection of erotica and sex

education books I had ever seen outside of a radical feminist bookstore. She said they were remnants from when she was a sex educator.

"Obviously there's a lot I don't know about you," I said. I got into her bed, instantly comfortable, wrapped in thick blankets, soft sheets and plush pillows.

"I sleep with lit candles. Is that okay?" Sy asked.

"This is your bedroom, girl. You do whatever you want."

"Be careful what you say, woman. Word is bond." She winked at me, and I smiled as she touched flame to candlewick.

coffee & cardamom

At midnight, Lee went to a twenty-four-hour gym in the Lower East Side and made her way to a basketball court. A place that was home to her. A place where she felt she was good at something.

She wore sweatpants and a hoodie hung low over her forehead. She hugged a basketball beneath her arm.

She dribbled.

From the three-point line, she shot free throw after free throw.

The stands were empty and the scoreboard on the other side of the court was off.

She didn't recognize herself anymore, didn't know if she liked herself anymore. She jogged up and down, vigorously dribbling the ball until her back and forehead were sweaty.

Lee couldn't stomach being home alone in the aftermath of what had happened. She felt nauseous. It had been three days since she'd seen Taylor and she'd made a point since then to be alone as little as possible. She tried to be around people to distract herself, but she didn't engage with them. She studied at the library, and randomly went to events, but hugged the wall, suddenly a wallflower. She went out and stayed out to avoid being by herself.

Her red sneakers squeaked against the shiny, freshly polished hardwood floor. The bright, fluorescent lights inside the gym belied the night outside. Thighs aching, biceps burning, breath heavy, she stopped shooting baskets and sat in the middle of the court. The basketball bounced and rolled away from her, its momentum slowing down as it got farther and farther away. Her arms formed a loose circle around her knees. She nervously bit the inside of her upper lip. Tears began streaming down her cheeks. She bowed her head between her knees and her shoulders shook gently.

She didn't wipe her tears away; just closed her eyes and let them come. She didn't know what to do and didn't understand who she was becoming. In that moment with Taylor she hadn't known how to stop herself. Something inside her had felt like uncontrollable thunder and she'd struck—Taylor.

She probably never wants to see me again.

Lee missed Taylor. Her heart ached with it.

Her nose and eyes were red. She leaned until her back was flat on the court. The clock on the wall read 1:45 a.m. Sniffling loudly, she got up and jogged over to the basketball, scooped it up and headed for the showers.

Clean and dressed, Lee entered the night. Cars and yellow taxies sped down 1st Avenue; pizza shops, bodegas and bars were open. Sirens wailed in the distance, a familiar nighttime melody. The night was busy enough to hide Lee. And she needed to feel hidden, needed to feel unseen. She walked to Breakfast, a tiny mom-and-pop spot in the Village that served breakfast all day, and had managed to stay put despite the recent, rapid gentrification of the neighborhood. She sat in a booth in the corner.

Lee's order arrived: thick French toast dusted with cardamom and drizzled with vanilla-infused maple syrup. Her coffee was black; the smell drifted up to her nose and soothed her a bit. She sipped it. It was strong and rich, exactly the way she liked it.

The French toast looked delicious, but she had no appetite. She didn't know why she'd ordered anything, or why she'd come.

Although … this *was* where she and Taylor had gone for their first date. Lee had been so nervous she'd spilled ice water all over their menus and table. Her face had burned with embarrassment and she'd admitted, "I'm clumsy when I'm nervous." Taylor had smiled and asked, "Why are you nervous?"

"I like you. And that … makes me nervous."

Tay had been so sweet; eyes looking away quickly, then looking back.

Lee felt tears welling up again, and blinked rapidly to lock them in. She let the sounds of the restaurant distract her—the scrape of chairs sliding against the floor, the clink of silverware hitting plates and the hum of indistinct conversations. Lee inhaled the sweet smells of her food and leaned her head forward into her open palms.

Opening her eyes, she breathed deeply.

This was Taylor's favorite dish at Breakfast.

She took a bite and found her appetite.

Lee let go in that moment. Her coffee was smooth liquid velvet down her throat, and she ate one bite of French toast after another.

She would call Taylor, even though she didn't have the right words to say. Because she needed to.

FOR SIZAKELE

hands

"Morning," Sy mumbled in a sexy, throaty voice.

That wasn't Lee's voice. And this *wasn't* Lee's body beside mine.

I opened my eyes quickly. "Mm-morning … um …" I started a half-hearted protest, but melted my back into the warm length of her body. *Protest to what?* Friends can spoon each other, I rationalized. I've held my friends before … *but holding them didn't make me want to turn around and lay my lips on their neck.*

I breathed in. "You okay?" she asked.

"Yeah, yeah I'm fine." My eyes focused on the picture of her mother on the wall in front of me. I smiled. They looked so much alike, both so beautiful; their eyes told stories of red soil, palm trees and a love of family. I reached for Sy's hand on my waist and held it for a second before I sat on the edge of her bed. I had wanted to put my lips to her hand; I had wanted to keep lying there. I breathed slowly.

Her bedroom in the daylight was a dream. Queen-sized bed, and a black dresser topped with a vanity mirror, a silver jewelry box and what looked like various scented oils.

Okay, so I obviously have a crush on this woman. I grabbed my neatly folded clothes from the top of her dresser and walked to the bathroom to change. I brushed my teeth with the toothbrush she'd left out for me. Early morning lethargy wrapped around me, making the crisp edges of the morning fuzzy. I looked in the mirror, wondering if I would be able to suppress my attraction to Sy. When I walked out of the bathroom, I looked into Sy's eyes for the first time since waking up. "Thank you for dinner and for letting me spend the night in your *incredibly* comfortable bed … and thank you for the sweet-smelling soaps and laughter."

"Anytime. Thank you for blessing me with your company." Sy's oversized nightshirt exposed her bare shoulder; she got out from under the covers and we hugged for a long time, then she walked me to the door.

I reveled in the early morning sounds of Brooklyn: the crunch of fresh snow mixed with salt beneath my feet, the *swoosh* of the buses passing by, and the protests of warmly bundled children as they ran behind mamas rushing to catch those buses. Hearing the distant rumble of an arriving train, I flew down the subway stairs, grabbed my MetroCard from my pocket, breezed through the turnstile and onto the platform in time to hop onto a Manhattan-bound A train. As the train moved through the underground labyrinth of the city, I smiled secretly at the memory of waking up beside Sy in her lush bed. I would have loved to linger longer in bed and talk about anything … nothing … something. I didn't want to spend time thinking about Lee and why it felt so good to be snuggled into Sy.

I exited the train at West 4th Street and headed for my dorm. Up on the second floor, I turned a corner and walked down the hall with my head bowed, trying to remember which pocket my room keycard was in. Two or three doors away from my room, I stopped mid-stride: Lee was looking up at me intently from the spot where she was sitting beside my door.

I swallowed and took a breath, then continued walking. I opened the door and she followed me in, as she had so many times before.

Lee cleared her throat. "Did you get my message?"

"No." I grabbed my phone from my back pocket. Looking at the screen, I saw notifications of a missed call and voicemail from her.

"I miss you." I turned and looked into Lee's eyes as I listened to the rest of her message. "I don't know where you are but I hope you're safe. Please call me when you get in." She paused. "I'm sorry about everything. I love you." The timestamp said she'd called at 3:03 a.m.

I guarded myself against feeling what I would naturally feel after not speaking with my girl for half a week. I resisted missing her and pushed aside my desire to kiss and hold her.

I tried to *not* care.

But I did.

"I was worried about you," Lee said softly.

I didn't say anything; I just stared at her. She moved closer to me from the other side of the room. I glanced at the bed—

Remembered.

"I really don't want to be alone with you in my room."

She looked surprised and caught off-guard. "But I need to talk to you. We can go somewhere else, can we go somewhere …? I just want to talk—"

There were tears behind my eyes. "Whatever." I jerked the door wide open so she could walk out first, then I followed.

"Where do you want to go?" she asked.

"It doesn't matter."

Shoving my hands in my back pockets, I walked next to her like she was a stranger, looking everywhere but at her, and keeping my distance so I'd feel safe. We went down the stairs and out the door.

"Do you want to go to the Paradise coffee spot?" Lee asked.

"Whatever."

We started walking.

"Taylor, I'm sorry."

I remained silent, playing with my tongue between my teeth to keep myself from screaming.

"Taylor?"

"What?" I barked.

"Aren't you gonna say anything?"

"No."

"Baby—"

"Don't—" I struggled to rein in my anger "—call me that."

"I know I was wrong. I was really jealous and I didn't

know how to handle… what I was feeling."

"I think it was a little more than jealousy."

"I—"

"You wanted to control me," I said. I turned to look at her. "Did it feel good?"

"No—"

I looked away. "You're lying."

"Taylor—"

"You would've stopped sooner if it didn't feel good."

The light turned yellow as I crossed St. Marks Place, but Lee hesitated and then it was too late for her to cross. When I reached the other side of the street, I looked back at her, above the cars whizzing by, then turned and kept walking into the wind.

Why am I even talking to her?

Paradise came up on my right, but I kept walking. Thoughts weren't forming properly in my head. I didn't know how to act, feel or be but I knew I was too agitated to sit down in a flippin café.

I felt a tentative hand on my shoulder. "I love you—"

I turned my head and stared at Lee's hand. I used to love looking at her hands because of the memories of how sweetly she'd made love to me, but now ... I saw them as a veiled threat. That scared me. And it angered me that I was scared. I shook her palm off.

"—very much and I—I lost control of myself. I was heated—I felt insecure because I thought you might be out with one of your boys or another woman. Then when you told me you were with Sy … I felt like I was losing my mind … losing you … losing my mind *because* I was losing you. I didn't want to hurt you but I didn't know how to talk about what I was feeling so I just—"

"—decided to use your physical power against me to teach me a lesson." Now I was facing her, in the middle of the sidewalk, in people's way.

"No—"

"*Yes,* and don't front."

I watched her hands move—straightening her shirt, scratching her forehead, cracking her knuckles. All her movements were at half-speed in my mind. I knew her hands were strong and could overpower me. Nothing felt the same. I knew we weren't on the same level of power. She had let me know.

"You don't trust me. You think I'm gonna leave you for a man any minute. You don't think I have the right to call myself a dyke because I'm bi. So why are you even with me?"

Lee looked pained. "Because I love you," she said, her voice aching.

I shrugged hard. "So?"

Her eyes widened with hurt.

"So what?" I said again, bolder than the first time. "What does your love do? Your love holds me down, hurts me and is too much of a coward to come see me until today." I sensed her anger, and continued. "And don't you dare get mad because you know it's true." I shook my head, disgusted. *She doesn't even feel me.* Looking all fucked up and sad, but *who* was crying so hard it hurt her body from the shaking?

That was *me.* Alone.

Why should I feel sorry for her for feeling bad when she *fucked up?*

"You're the only woman I've ever wanted to spend my life with," she said. My heart jumped, despite my anger. I deliberately looked down at the cracks in the sidewalk to avoid her eyes. "I know it—I know I was fucked up. I didn't even know I was hurting you, at the time—"

"How could you not know? I told you to stop."

"I … I lost control and I didn't know what to do. I don't want to hurt you again and I *won't.*"

My hands were stuffed in the pockets of my jean jacket, the tip of my right foot hitting the concrete over and over and over and—

Lee touched my cheek, sending an electric shock through me, and I reflexively pulled away. I couldn't look into her eyes.

"Are you through with me, Taylor?" she asked.

"I don't know."

She moved slightly closer. "I … I don't want to be without you." Her voice was softer.

I continued to look away.

"Aren't you gonna say anything?"

"What's there for me to say?" I asked, finally shifting my gaze back to her. "You need to stop sugar-coating shit like I'm stupid. Any dumbass can figure out that what happened was fucked up, but *why* did it happen, *how* could you let that happen? How could you do that to me? *To me, Lee!*" I blinked fast to keep tears in, then shut up to stop my voice from quivering.

Lee sighed. "I wanted to feel as if there was something I had control over … in regards to you. You're the busiest woman I know … and sometimes you come home too tired to even talk to me. I feel like you don't need me and will leave me. I wanted your attention."

"Maybe next time, you can just say, 'Hey, Taylor, pay me some attention!' What the fuck is wrong with you?"

"I—"

"Go ahead and justify yourself some more, find some excuse to explain how you distorted your love into hate to do that to me." My voice was cracking, and people were staring; I didn't care. "I like attention, too but I don't—" I stopped myself before I lost it.

She bowed her head, biting her lip, shoulders sagging. "I'm sorry, I'm *so* sorry. Baby, I miss you."

We were silent as minutes slowly ticked by. My anger was heavy, and I was tired of holding it up, tired of the energy it took to feel it.

She whispered so low the wind almost stole her words. "Tay … can I hold you?"

She asked me,
she asked …
how precious lee late but
sweet.

I looked into her eyes and let her see my tears. "Fuck you."

"I love you." Her eyes searched mine. *"I love you."*

I grabbed her face; her tongue, our lips, her firm fingertips hot on my neck. It felt like a new old kiss. I wanted to let my body shake from the hunger that had developed in me from missing her but I made myself still.

I'd missed her. *I still love—*

ꕥ

Her hands held and caressed me, but I could not let her make love to my body. Even though cuddling felt good, somehow sleeping with Lee didn't feel right, didn't feel like it used to. I used to feel protected, but now it was her I felt I needed protection from. Maybe I was being dramatic; maybe it wasn't that big of a deal. Why keep going over it in my head? *Hands pressed into my wrists, my balled up fists, holding me down a power trip too good to resist* … But it *was* a big deal and I couldn't let it go. So I slept alone that night.

The next morning I headed to work, cleaning my professor's apartment. I took my Aretha Franklin mixtape with me. I *loved* that she still had a working tape deck and record player. I snapped the mix into the tape deck and pressed the faded play button. My shoulders loosened the minute I heard Aretha's voice fill and bless the space. I let my bag drop onto her leather couch, then I let *me* drop onto the couch. I was always fascinated by my professor's apartment: the crystal figurines; the ornate, antique vanity mirror in the bedroom; the grand piano; the oak coffee table; and the bar lined with bottles of blackberry brandy, wine, and glistening wine and shot glasses. The huge ceiling-to-floor window in the living room faced campus, and I could see busy students rushing everywhere.

Aretha sang and her voice shook me from the inside. I slowly rolled up my sleeves, feeling the "my-baby-just-left-me" blues. The granddaddy clock read 9:30 a.m. or rather 9:30 w.m.t. (white man's time, as I sometimes called it). I reluctantly pushed myself up: time to clean.

I started with the kitchen, which thankfully wasn't that bad. I did the dishes, mopped the floor and wiped down all the surfaces with a bleach-and-lemon-scented disinfectant. Next the living room, then the bedroom—I made the bed, vacuumed, tidied up, then cleaned the adjoining bathroom for which I broke out the rubber gloves. I scrubbed the tub, mopped the floor, cleaned the toilet. I slid out my tape, picked up my things and slowly, thoughtfully picked up my $100 payment from the side table by the door. I turned around and admired my work. Nice. Done in two hours. Locking the door behind me, I headed back to my dorm to shower and get all the gunk off me. Cleaning made me feel dirty.

The rest of the day I walked around on the verge of tears, just *feeling* it.

She apologized. So everything is okay now … right?

Times like this made me want to adopt some sort of unhealthy coping device to get through, to get by, to live and breathe through days like this.

The friends and acquaintances I ran into spoke to me from the same script: *Hey Taylor, what's up, how're you, missed you the past couple days, where you been, see you later, call me, I love you, you okay? Are you okay? Do you wanna talk?*

Yeah I'm fine/you turned around just in time/to miss my eyes rain.

FOR SIZAKELE

the sky cries for me

A sharp honk behind me made me jump. It was dusk and misty, and the daytime rush of students going to and from classes had lessened. My heartbeat quickened as I watched a black SUV drive toward me. I thought I heard someone from inside the car yell my name, but the voice was too muffled for me to recognize it.

The car slowed to a stop and the driver's side window rolled down.

Dani!

I looked her up and down, side to side. I hadn't seen my homegirl since spending last summer in Detroit. I'd stumbled onto her '90s R&B dance class and loved it; we became instant friends. Her pencil-thin dreads had grown a couple inches longer since then and tumbled over her left shoulder. Her brown skin looked flawless and her eyes were warm. She looked amazing.

"I can't believe you're here!" I said.

Dani hopped out of the car and hugged me. "Why not?" She smiled widely, her hand shielding her face against the light drizzle.

"Because I haven't seen you in *so* long! Nice car. Boss shit!"

Dani laughed. "Thanks, it's a rental. The dancers and I are on tour and we're driving from city to city."

"Congratulations!" She reached for my face, making a gentle semi-circle under each of my eyes with her fingers. "Haven't you been sleeping enough? There are circles under your eyes."

"I'm just tired."

Dani looked at me, clearly doubting my answer. "Get in the car, let's go somewhere and talk about it."

We got in the car and Dani adjusted the rearview mirror.

The drizzle turned to rain. "Now tell me what's making you look so sad," Dani said.

"No, please, I wanna talk about what you've been up to since—"

"All that shit can wait. Talk." She put the car in gear.

Dani never let me hide. I clicked my seatbelt into place. "It's me and Lee... We just made up after a fight and things aren't the same. No matter what I say to myself, I can't relax with her. I don't even look forward to being in her arms anymore."

"What'd you fight over?"

"She held me down in bed when I told her to stop. And she put her hand around my throat."

"She *what?*"

"That's why we weren't speaking for awhile. Now I don't know how to love her. I mean of course I *love* her, but I don't know how to be vulnerable with her because she made me feel so weak. I don't trust her anymore."

"Taylor, this is bananas, you don't need this shit!"

"I know I don't. Lee *was* my baby. We talked yesterday morning, and not that much time has passed since then, so maybe I'm overanalyzing everything too soon but..."

"But what, sweetie?"

"It doesn't feel the same. Lee was my haven, my hideaway, my *rock*. Now I'm on guard like I can't be myself with her because she might hurt me."

Driving at night was soothing. The night was a black blanket, and the darkness made me feel safe and anonymous. Dani knew exactly what to do—just drive and drive like we used to in Detroit, and we'd end up wherever we ended up. I'd missed our beautiful moments.

"Even now, everything wouldn't seem half as bad if I knew I could go home and just lay with her. I know I sound mad corny but she always made everything seem better."

The windshield wipers danced a sexy dance against the windshield—back and forth, retreating and progressing. It was a seduction—like here I am, here I'm not. It was funny, because though the wipers were in sync, they never touched. Their dance always fascinated me. *What if Lee and me had lost* it, *lost the spark, the connection that made us an "us"? How were we supposed to recover from this?*

"I've never seen you like this," Dani said.

"Like what?"

"I've never seen you this … unhappy," she said softly. "I can see that you really love her."

"Have you ever—" I stopped.

"What?"

"Have you ever loved someone so much it became scary? Like one argument with them and something inside you shifts—is offset? This can't be normal. This is beyond depressed. This sadness has sunk … into my soul. I can't even look my friends in the eye because I don't want them to see the part of me that's missing, that's still with Lee." I shook my head and watched the rain slide down the passenger window. Raindrop families chased each other.

"It hurts a lot," I said.

Dani pulled onto the side of the road. We sat and listened to the rain together. We were both hypnotized by the sounds around us—the sounds of the rain were a song: the steady beat of rain on the car was the bass line and the windshield wipers' squeaky *sliiide* and muted *click* were the heartbeat of the song. Dani ran her manicured fingers absently along the steering wheel, deliberate and slow as if the soft wheel were something else, maybe someone … then she stopped and gripped it tightly. Sadness washed over her face.

"Tay, I understand being so wrapped up in someone that they have an itch and you reach to scratch it on your own body; yes, I understand that. That sort of connection is as frightening as it is amazing." She paused and breathed deeply, like she was searching for some strength, the right words, or both. "I understand what it's like when that person and you are out of sync, are fighting with each other or hurting each other. The last woman I was with—" Dani laughed. "Sometimes I think she'll be the last woman I'm *ever* with. I more than loved her; I wanted to *be* her sometimes so that she wouldn't have to live through any pain. We broke up but we're still together. I can *feel* her."

"I don't know how I would deal with that—with not being with Lee but still having her in my heart and head," I said. "I don't *want* to have to figure out how to move on or be without her. I want us to work but *damn,* she was so wrong for what she did and I'm angrier at her than I have ever been at anyone. I see her and everything is defined by that anger. I kiss her and I want her, I'm attracted to her but then I'm mad that her body still feels good to me. That's why I didn't spend the night with her last night. I've been so out of it today. The first words out of the mouth of everyone I've spoken to today has been 'what's wrong' or 'are you okay.' And I lie to them, but no, I'm *not* okay and everything feels fuckin *wrong.* If Lee and I aren't on point, then everything else is on shaky ground."

Dani's hands caressed the steering wheel. "Ma, I've got to say this to you. No matter how much you love someone, you can never lose yourself in them. You can never wrap yourself up in them, and who you are together, to the point that who you are by yourself doesn't matter or is forgotten. I'm not saying you did that. I'm saying it because I think that I lost myself in my ex. I lost myself right there in the iris of her eyes. I let myself live within her vision of who I should be and pushed down into the pit of myself who I knew I was." She sighed. "There's a million ways to get lost. You can get lost the way I did or you can get lost within your coupleness to the point you don't really think about you as an individual anymore. You ignore your own needs and then if you fight or if something threatens that coupleness you start losing your damn mind. I see this …" She looked over at me. "I see this throbbing *ache* in your eyes and it reminds me *of* me. You said y'all made up since when?"

"Yesterday morning."

"Have the two of you sat down and talked everything through?"

"No. When I came home she was there waiting for me and we took a walk and talked a little bit, but we haven't talked since then. I've been avoiding her."

"Well, no wonder nothing is sorted out. You haven't had the chance to go over what happened, what it means and really hold her accountable for what she did."

"I don't know if I'm ready—or if I can."

"Is it that you can't deal with this right now? Or that you choose not to?"

"Yes and yes." I laughed hollowly. "I need time and space to figure it out. But I didn't want us not speaking to each other at all while I'm figuring all this shit out."

"Did you tell her that?"

"No. She held me down. I don't owe her shit."

"Did you take her back?"

I wanted to defiantly spit out "fuck no" but I couldn't. That had been me on St. Mark's Place yesterday, right? I had opened my arms to her and I had let her kiss be a force strong enough to pull a door open in me that her holding me down had slammed shut. After all the bullshit, that door was open again. Just a crack, but it was open.

"Yeah, I took her back."

"You're more forgiving than me. You're still committed to the both of you being together then? On some level?"

"I guess."

"Taylor, be honest with yourself." She wasn't gonna let me get away with my half-assed answer.

"Alright, *yes,* I'm committed," I said. "I feel like having one foot in and one foot out right now."

"I understand why you're angry. Obviously Lee does too or she wouldn't have felt the need to apologize, but it seems like you don't want to be open, or aren't ready to open up about how angry you really are. I think *furious* might be a better word."

"I don't want to talk about it with her."

"She's your girlfriend."

"So? She's the reason for all this. I'm too angry to deal with my anger, let alone with her. It's rooted so deep inside me, I want to break shit. I can't believe she—" I started trembling and had to stop talking. My heart beat faster as if Lee was on top of me again. I clenched my fists and inhaled sharply, shutting my eyes and trying to calm myself.

"Taylor?" Dani said.

"Yeah?"

"Are you okay?"

"No," I said.

"I'm really worried about you."

"Dani, I'm worried about me too."

3:39 a.m.

I got off the A train at Utica Avenue and headed to Lee's. With every few steps I took, a new thought or an old memory entered my mind. Dani's words still bounced around in my head. Snapshots of Lee and me flashed through my head.

Snapshot: Lee and me tumbling out of the elevator, coming home late after her teammate's birthday party.

Snapshot: Her holding my hand before a performance, whispering, *"Baby, you got this."*

Snapshot: The day she gave me keys to her apartment and said, *"This is our place."*

At 3:39 a.m. I found myself … no, I had *brought* myself here, in front of Lee's door, to see if it was still ours. I turned my key, gently pushed the door open and shut it carefully behind me. I slowly dropped my bag and coat to the carpet. I left the lights off and let my eyes adjust to the darkness of the living room I'd spent so much time in—studying, being distracted from studying by Lee's fine self, or yelling my half of our conversations from the couch to Lee, who might have been in any room. I hesitated as the memories cascaded into my heart and mind.

What's wrong?

But I knew what was wrong. Nothing was the same between us anymore.

I slowly took off all my clothes, leaving them in a small tumble of a mess outside the bedroom door. With only my panties on, I tiptoed into the room and saw Lee sleeping, heard her breathing softly. I slipped under the covers and ran my hands over her hips; our bodies found each other's curves with the ease of lovers familiar with each other. Lee groaned in her sleep.

"Baby …?" she mumbled.

"Yes?"

"When'd you get here?"

"Just now."

"Oh …"

My heart jumped. "You want me to leave?"

"Nono …" she said sleepily. "I just … I just thought you didn't wanna sleep with me."

The simple way she said that gave me heartache-coated pause.

"I … missed you," I said.

She pulled me closer to her and snuggled her head into my neck, wrapping her arms around me firmly. She began to kiss my neck and I arched it; I extended my leg over her body as her hands ran sensually up and down my back. I hungered for her lips, lips that were traveling down my chest, sucking on me. She was on top of me now; I tugged her shirt over her head and pulled her bare chest down onto mine, sighing at the feel of her hard nipples on mine. I wanted to talk to her, to tell her how her body was making me feel, but I couldn't.

There was sand in my throat,
thieves on my tongue
running away with my voice.

Wrapping my arms around her, I grinded on her slowly … like foreplay, like getting to know her again. We kissed and it was like yesterday. I mean like *yesterdayyesterday.* Sucking, biting, licking … *kissing like yesterday.* Her hands caressed up and down my sides, down to my thighs, squeezing and teasing, then her fingers wandered to the inside of my thighs and I stopped breathing. She gently took my panties off and I started breathing faster in anticipation.

"Taylor?"

"Huh?"

"Is everything okay?"

"Hmm-mm, yesyes, *please* ..."

"Okay, baby ..."

"Jeje."

"What?"

"Be gentle."

When her fingers touched my pussy something in me was released and I almost came: just from that. Somewhere behind my eyes I wanted to let something go, but it felt too far to be tears; close enough, though, to be recognized as fears. Lee caressed my clit slowly, very slowly, with excruciating softness until my breathing became jagged. Just as she went to slip her fingers inside me, I grabbed her wrist.

"What's wrong?"

"I don't know," I said, fast and honest. "I'm scared."

"Why?"

"I don't know. I don't want you—to—hurt me."

"I would never ... I would never hurt you. Taylor. *Baby* ..." She eased her hand out of my grip and placed her palm on the side of my thigh in a gesture I know was meant to comfort me, but I involuntarily tensed anyway.

She pulled her palm away. "You don't trust me?"

I let my eyes caress the only woman I had ever felt comfortable calling my love. The body I had kissed, rode, been inside of, that had been on top of and beside me; the body that brought me to breathlessness and weakness and speechlessness. *Such a beautiful body ...*

"You *don't* trust me," she said, and dropped her eyes.

"Don't do that, don't sound like that." My heart twisted into a painful pretzel.

"I can't believe I let this happen to us." She lifted her head and looked sad. "I want to make you feel precious. And good."

"Lee ..." I hesitated. "I don't even know if I should finish my thought out loud."

"Why not?"

"It's hard for me to share my feelings because I know that

makes me vulnerable in a way I can't take back," I said.

"But it's just me."

"I know that, but who you are and what you feel isn't so clear anymore."

She nodded. "So I have to show you …"

"Yes. I miss you, I want you … I really want to make love to you," I said. "But it might hurt." The tears behind my eyes were creeping closer. "Maybe you don't know how much I love you"—and closer— "but I do, and I don't want you to hurt me. I can't be a weak little femme tonight."

"Taylor, you've *never* been a weak little femme."

"Maybe not. But I've felt like one."

I slid from underneath her and lay on my side with my back to her.

"Should I—can I touch you?"

I mouthed *yes*, but said, "No."

Yes *because I want you but* no *because I can't want you right now.*

ଔଷ

We drifted into a fitful sleep under a blanket of tense silence, lovers laying side by side yet not touching, not cuddling, not laughing, not even kissing good night. Such a travesty of love.

I was very conscious of my nakedness. I couldn't fall back into who I was and who we were together. I needed to understand what my strength was as a dyke, a femme dyke, and be comfortable with that—even outside of the jurisdiction of our relationship and outside of relating to Lee as my soft butch woman. I couldn't let the only way I thought about my own gender identity be just in relation to Lee's masculinity, because then all I could ever be was confined to who she *was* or *wasn't*. I needed to figure out my own femininity on my own terms.

I didn't sleep well and I didn't sleep much. I woke up several times that night; the last time my eyes opened I just kept them open, got dressed and left.

It was 7 a.m.; I didn't have class till 1 p.m. Today was supposed to be one of the few days that I could sleep in, but I didn't want to talk to Lee or deal with what was between us, so I forfeited sleep for peace of mind.

An early morning haze hung in the air, a remnant from last night's rain; as the moisture in the air sunk into my skin, I replayed the night before in my head, wanting to truly know what had made me stop her. It had felt *so fucking good* and I had needed so badly to be made love to in the gentle, perfect, selfless way she used to—but I just couldn't let her inside me. I couldn't give myself up to her, over to her; I couldn't let go enough to let that happen.

Maybe I shouldn't have even gone over to her apartment, maybe I should have kept myself under control, maybe I should have kept my clothes on—I didn't know what was the right "should" to abide by. Going over to Lee's was not about lust; it was about me missing her. But making love with her could never be as simple as it once was. I knew that if I let her make me come, that meant I would have to trust her and open myself up to her and she would be in control—that control that comes from having the pinnacle of your lover's pleasure on your fingertips, or between your lips, or within the thrust or grind of your hips. Never before had I thought of sex in terms of control and who had it over whom, but now I couldn't help it. Images of my body on top of Lee's flashed into my head, snippets of her face—eyes closed, mouth open, moaning and needing me. Though I'd left Lee that morning for peace of mind, each piece of my mind was engulfed in thoughts of her.

Whereas Lee and I used to share power and have a mutually fulfilling sex life, now I couldn't give her any power over me. I had to have it all and that meant I couldn't let her touch me anymore.

I got back to my dorm and showered. *Maybe I should've left a note, should've said goodbye, shouldn't have left at all, should call to say … something, even if I really said nothing much once she was on the line.* Then again, maybe I should do what makes me feel whole inside, even if I have to hurt her. I didn't want to hurt her but it hurt me when I tried so hard to *not* hurt her, and what about me?

Who's gonna take away my hurt but *me?*

ೞ

I guess Lee knew me well enough to know not to call. She didn't call or text, and thankfully I didn't run into her. I needed time to think. Usually she'd meet me after my last class of the day and we'd go eat or chill, but not today. The broken routine made me feel lonely.

Over the next couple weeks, I found it more and more difficult to open up to Lee about anything, especially if I needed comfort, advice or support—so I didn't. It showed, and we both felt it.

Eventually I started touching Lee's body out of habit. I let myself believe that if I did it for long enough it would feel like it used to.

One Sunday afternoon lying in her bed, Lee asked, "Why can't I touch you?"

"You're touching me right now," I said. I fluffed the pillow behind my head.

"Taylor, you know that's not what I mean. Why won't you let me top you anymore?"

"Because I don't want you to." I ignored the look of pain on her face.

"Baby, I want to make love to you, I want to please you the way—"

"Stop. Stop it!" I snapped. "I don't want to hear it."

Because I start to remember the pleasure, but right now I want to remember the pain.

Fucking was a battlefield and our bed was a war zone.

I needed to feel in control of my body and the sex I had. I'd started making love and fuckin with my bra and panties on, to be as untouchable as possible, literally.

I didn't want to wear tight-fitting clothes or paint my nails anymore. My jeans hung a little lower on my hips, material slightly loose around my legs. I wore T-shirts one size too big, or a hoodie. I needed a buffer between my body and the world, between my body and Lee's body.

These clothes were my fort and my harbor; I needed a place to breathe, a place to distance myself from how I'd felt when Lee held me down. I rested within my own masculinity and in the folds of these looser clothes. I found a way, in the nuances of exploring my own gender, to take a reprieve from feeling vulnerable.

Femininity isn't weak. But given that I'd been expressing my gender as femme and feminine when Lee held me down, I just needed to be … *not* feminine. For awhile.

I wasn't ready to walk away from her and I wasn't ready to let her back in, so I was stuck in the in-between, languishing and confined within this non-intimacy.

Even though I wanted to be held, I refused to let her touch, comfort or please me. Because I didn't feel safe enough to. I was never on the bottom anymore; I always made the first move sexually and I rarely slept over. I'd started pulling away sexually to prove something to myself and I'd forgotten if I had the evidence I needed or if I was becoming someone I didn't want to be, running from intimacy by pretending I was perpetually in control.

"Taylor …" she started talking again in that voice, that voice that irritated the fuck out of me … that sweet "I'm sorry, let's talk" voice.

"Yeah?" I answered flatly, turning to face the wall. My mind pushed past half-open curtains and jumped out the window. I wondered about the people walking past the apartment building. Did that woman with the pink head wrap want to scream in bed at her lover in rage even in the midst of passion, like I do? Did the pecan brown woman with the kicks to match the jacket to match the hat every day shut her beloved out of her heart because she couldn't trust her with her vulnerable and delicate parts? Did the queer man with impeccable hair and spotless boots run from the stories inside him that he couldn't name or understand?

"Taylor—" She placed a hesitant hand on my waist. I tensed and slipped out of bed. "What's wrong?" she asked.

"Nothing."

"Then why are you getting up?"

"I don't feel like lying in bed anymore."

"Taylor, we don't talk anymore."

"What do you want to talk about?"

"Why you've shut me out."

I threw the words at her with thinly veiled resentment. "Why I've shut you out is *because* you don't know why I'd want to."

FOR SIZAKELE

whole body a wound

I locked & bolted the door
barricaded myself in
& begged you
come in

this body I'm in
behind this barricade
sometimes triggers me,
shouts loud stories I want to forget
at decibels I cannot mute.

my own reflection
betrays me with memories
where your hands ground into the soft of me
I remember
just by looking at me
I remember
that
which ripped me
apart

whole body
a wound

I cover me up,
clothes serve as bandage,
splint,
makeshift
surgery

YVONNE FLY ONAKEME ETAGHENE

in my mirror
my arms are landmines
my exposed breasts are explosives
my hips be TNT

sometimes
I hide
        the soft me
in other
        harder
places

for awhile

to forget

sista to sista o

A.C.,
How you dey, sista? I'm emailing you a little bit at a loss. I know you said to keep in touch and I know you meant it so here I am. Lately I feel like my heart and I got a divorce but I'm only now finding out about it. I've shut down. My girlfriend is constantly trying to connect with me and I never wanna deal with her feelings. Some violence happened between us—enacted on me by her and now I feel such rage. I don't know how to be soft with her anymore. I'm unhappy and pissed *all the time*. I can't see Lee (that's my girlfriend) as this amazing, beautiful person—all she is to me is that asshole that fucked me over.

A.C., I feel like I can't breathe, and I don't know what to do about that.

I feel myself becoming the kind of stone butch I've always been annoyed with and criticized. Don't get it twisted—I love all varieties of butch expression and there is nothing wrong with being stone, and if my gender identity is shifting then cool, I'll roll with it, but what I really feel is happening is I'm using butchness as armor to protect myself from Lee, and to make her feel vulnerable while I choose *not* to be vulnerable and maintain as much control as possible. Somewhere in butchness, masculinity and baggy clothes is this comforting place for me to hide my hurt. When I've dated women who used being stone as an excuse to be emotionally unavailable, it aggravated the shit out of me—and now I'm doing that exact same fuckin thing. I can intellectualize the fuck out of what's goin on with me and Lee, but I still feel fuckin stuck and I still feel like shit.

Annnnd, I'm thinking about changing my major. Did I mention I'm a second semester sophomore? This is so NOT the time to switch boats midstream (I think I just botched that metaphor). Creative Writing feels more in line with what I want to do after college than an English degree. Or maybe Comparative Literature. I just wanna read pretty, thoughtful words then write pretty, thoughtful words about what I read. Is there a fancy degree that will let me do that?

sigh I know this is a lot and I hope it's not overwhelming. I hope you're well—in fact, I hope you feel fuckin phenomenal. You're such an inspiration to me and I'm honored to know you.

Sending Love,
*Ejiroghene

FOR SIZAKELE

Oghene, my sista o!

shit, i'm so sorry to hear that you're dealin with so much! it sounds hella hectic. regarding your major, you gotta do what feels right, even if it seems inconvenient. the last thing you want is a degree in something you don't care about.

it's hard to be with someone, to love them and be good to them as you love and be good to your damn self too. on top of that, dealin with violence and what sounds like abuse? my dear sista o, please think about what you can hold. maybe you need a break from each other? i know us dykes like to process and talk … and then talk about the talk and process (lol) but sometimes you just need to breathe and take time for *you.* i'm a little worried about you—we didn't spend much time together while i was in NYC but i get the workaholic vibe from you. don't be offended—it takes one to know one! ;)

butchness is a nice place to hide your emotions, at times, more secure than a bank safety deposit box. i've tucked my emotions into butchness many times. it's an easy hiding place, because when we're looking for emotions, who would ever expect a butch to be caging vulnerability inside her? i am sometimes guilty of this and work every day to be brave enough to be vulnerable with my lover. fuck what *any* of us heard, butch and vulnerable can and do co-exist beautifully in the same heart, body and spirit.

i wanna give you the miracle formula to ease your heart and soothe you, but i don't have one. all i can say is listen to what your soul is telling you and *follow that instruction no matter how difficult or doubtful you are of the message.* lee did what she did and none of your rage is gonna change that—don't allow yourself to be stuck in an incident that does not empower you. learn what you need to learn but don't allow yourself to be immobilized by your rage. feel your rage, of course, just please don't get stuck in it. i don't *at all* mean to sound preachy! all this advice comes from my heart, from my own experience of figuring out how to love again after being hurt/violated/dishonored. it's a process that takes time, prayer, poetry, tenderness, breath then *more time, more prayer, more poetry, more tenderness, more breath, more breath, more breath, more breath.*

i will do my best to hold your spirit up all the way from oaktown. you have my number, use it.

tare always!
A to tha C

engendering surrender

"What up, Miss Invisible? It's Tatiyana. You must have transferred to another school, or left the country maybe? Because I know *that's the only way you'd be this out of touch with me. I haven't seen you in a month! Are you still tormented over Lee and isolating yourself in depression? That is so '80s-movie tortured melodrama. Return my call or I'm gonna show up on your doorstep and make you laugh if it takes all night. Holla at your girl."*

I had to laugh at Tati's hilarious voicemail. I sighed, knowing I would have to answer the inevitable "how are you?" I didn't know if I was up for it but I called. Because it was Tati.

"Hi Tati," I said, leaning back against my bed pillows.

"Oh my God, *thank* God. Where the hell have you been?"

"Feelin like shit, skipping class and sleeping a lot."

"That sounds healthy."

"*Please* don't judge me. I can't take it right now."

"Querida, I'm teasing you. Damn, girl, talk to me."

"My entire relationship with Lee has fallen to shit and I don't know how to fix it. We're barely having real conversations and when we *do* talk, we fight."

"What do you fight about?"

"Nothing, everything. Lately she's hella jealous of my friendship with Sy."

"*Friendship?* Um, that sounds like a bit of creative fiction."

"What are you talking about?"

"Have you slept with her yet?"

"Tatiyana! Do you *really* think I'm that grimy?"

"Sy is *fine*. The word 'grimy' does not come to mind when I think of the two of you."

"I really don't need to hear this right now." I sighed heavily.

"Taylor, I'm teasing you! I miss playing around with you.

Lo siento, ma, I don't mean to be insensitive. What I mean is I've seen how the two of you are with each other when you drop by Sweeter. Sy makes you smile like I've never seen you smile and that's beautiful to see. From where I sit, it looks like a little bit more than a friendship."

I rolled my eyes. "We're just friends, Tati."

"So you're not attracted to her?"

"She's beautiful!" I picked at my nails.

"Uh-huh, that's great, pero that's not what I asked you, mami. I asked if you're *attracted* to her."

I hesitated a little too long. "Okay, since it's clear that you want her, I say go for it." I had to laugh. I was only annoyed because Tatiyana was saying shit that I didn't want to admit … *might* be true. (Okay: *was true.*)

"You're honestly advising me to cheat on my girlfriend with my good friend? Are you *serious?*"

"Pretty much."

"You're fuckin bananas."

"I mean, are you monogamous with Lee?"

"Yes!"

"Ohhh …" She seemed genuinely puzzled. "Whose idea was that?"

I burst out laughing. "Do you know how ridiculous you are?"

"How are you supposed to get with Sy? *Hmm* … maybe it's time to have that, 'Let's see other people and still date each other' conversación?"

Tatiyana ain't no punk when it comes to loving her friends full out. She refused to let me just say goodbye at the end of our conversation and return to certain melancholy for the rest of my day/week/month; she insisted we meet up that night and catch up *for real for real.* "And then maybe some dancing till the early morn like we used to before you disappeared from the social scene?"

"Just come over and pick me up before I bury myself

under my covers and call it a night."

"I'm leaving now and you better be ready when I get there!"

ଓଃ୬

I opened my door to Tati's sweet face. She was rockin her beautifully weathered sienna brown leather jacket and a violet-colored hoodie underneath. And if I knew my homegirl, undoubtedly there was a muscle shirt beneath that. Her cowgirl boots peeked out of the bottom of straight-leg jeans. Tatiyana's Afro-Cuban-raised-in-Santa-Fe-behind rocked belts like a Texan in Brooklyn with no hesitation. The woman was *fierce.*

We hugged, and I pulled back to look at her again. "Nice eyeliner," I said, teasing. She knew she looked good.

"Tell me why this femmey girl from Obayemi's class—"

"Are you going to tell me something amazing about Obayemi again? I wanna hop over to the New School with you just to take *all* her classes." I led her inside my room so we could talk.

"She's pretty amazing. Maybe you can take a course next semester and have it transfer over to NYU?"

"Maybe. For now though, I don't know how the fuck I'm going to get through my midterms. I have two papers due this week that I haven't even started. But I don't even wanna *think* about that right now. Anyway, keep telling me your story. Femmey girl ...?"

"Yeah, so this femme was surprised to see my ass with eyeliner on last week. Like it's violating the Dyke Code of Conduct or some shit. I swear, some twisted people are on the committee that makes up these rules we're all supposed to live by. So I asked her if she was *so* femme, why wasn't she wearing a rib-breaking corset, too-tight stilettos and sitting at home playing wifey for some butch? She stood there looking confused and I walked away before she figured out I was insulting her. Those are the same women who are surprised when after I make love to them, I start telling them how I like my pussy ate. They're all shocked and shit, like just because I ride a motorcycle I don't want to be fucked. *Please*."

Tatiyana's candor never ceased to amaze me—and send me into a fit of giggles. Laughing, I said, "Girl, if you run into the femmes that expect a stone butch, I run into the butches who think just because I occasionally rock acrylic nails, I'm a pillow princess. Umm, what do my hands have to do with my strap and my tongue?"

"Word!" Tatiyana sat down on top of the hamper beside my closet. "That's what I'm saying. That's why I'm sick of labels. I used to be all about *'I'm butch, yadda ya, look at me.'* Now, fuck it, I'm just Tatiyana. If you wanna know what I check on the census, I don't check *shit* next to sexual orientation, I write in 'BULLDAGGER with a femmey swagger.'" She smiled and flipped her microbraids over her shoulder in an exaggerated gesture of her femininity.

"You betta serve that shampoo commercial realness!"

I loved the butchness of Tatiyana: I loved that her mechanic-I-can-fix-anything loveliness was so gentle with me and would just as quick throw on a super-duper-high-femmed-out pastel-colored apron and bake the most divinely sweet pies and cakes. She said it was the Donna Reed in her that had to bake with an apron that girly.

Tati turned serious. "Talk to me, mami. I haven't seen you in weeks."

"Well ... these days I have this love/hate relationship with Lee's butchness. All the qualities I loved about her, I now resent: her masculinity, her physical strength, her body. I can't trust any of it. I can't trust *her.* And I'm not saying physical strength is only masculine because of course it's not; of course feminine folks are strong, too. When she was holding me down, though, I felt like she was a man—a woman-hating, sexist man. I couldn't feel *her* anymore."

"I wonder if she could even feel herself in that moment," Tati said. "Gender is such a mind-fuck. You know I'm in Obayemi's 'Gender Fuck' class this semester?" I nodded. "Our community, our gender-fluid dyke asses, are gender *renegades.* Masculine characteristics are not isolated to men, just like feminine characteristics are not isolated to women. Pero when we start power-tripping and stop asking ourselves why we're acting a certain way—that's dangerous. And I ain't trying to see you get caught up in the crossfire of that gender battle."

"I already am. There are nights I lay in that bed with Lee and I don't even know who I am, Tati. Some nights, I lay there resenting her. I *never* let her top me anymore. My way of being strong is to keep her from giving me pleasure. I don't let myself surrender to her."

"'Surrender'? Like loser in a war?"

Interesting, my choice of words.

"I mean surrender, like be vulnerable," I said. "It's not only physical intimacy I'm hoarding to myself; it's emotional shit, too. I can't even remember the last time I went to her for advice or shared something sacred with her."

"I am resisting all my urges to kick Lee's ass for the fucked up shit she did to you," Tati said. "That's not me treating you like property; you're just my girl, and I love you. I don't want anyone treating you like that."

"I know," I said quietly.

"It kills me that she's hurting you like this. *Butch does not equal violence.* You shouldn't have to have your guard up in bed con su *amante.*"

"Amante?"

"Lover."

"I need to stop making love ... I can't even call it that anymore ... I have to stop having sex with her. I need to stop using sex as a space to exact my revenge, my anger. I need a break from her, from us, from *everything.*"

"Let me know what you need. Anything I can do, you

know I will in half a heartbeat."

"What I need is to *please* talk about what's up with you," I said, shifting gears. "Whose heart you breakin these days?"

"Me? Please. The player in me is retired."

"You're lying!"

"Girl, who has the time to remember everyone's names, hobbies and addresses?"

"Are you for real?"

"Dead ass. I really am. Over the last few months, I started thinking about why I was even juggling tres mujeres. The mornings after were the *worst*. Real talk, it all felt pointless in the daylight—the chase, the flirting, all to end up on my back trying to find the most polite way to say 'adiós, mi amor.'"

"So you're monogamous now?"

"Hey, hey, not so fast!" She laughed. "I'm… slowing down. I'm considering dating instead of just randomly hooking up."

"Is there a specific person—"

"Montana."

"Homegirl from Oakland who rolls with that b-girl crew?"

"Uh-huh."

"You like em hard, huh?"

"Only on the outside. Soft and gushy on the inside like me."

ꕥ

Tatiyana and me caught the sweetest of spirits on that dance floor till the daylight. The DJ killed it to *life*. Dancing, I felt reborn—stomping, jumping and pushing pain out of my pores. It was amazing to feel the music like it was my heartbeat, soul beat, life force up in me, loving my heart alive again. Neither one of us got tired; we just danced and danced and danced and … loved each other like only sisters can.

On the train ride home, I lay my head on Tati's shoulder and she wrapped her arm around me.

Sisterhood.

rage

"Could you shut the fuck up, Lee?"

Lee's shoulders sagged, already defeated. These days, Taylor's anger was a palpable force in most of their conversations and Lee didn't know what to do about it.

"What is fuckin wrong with you, Taylor?" Lee asked with a sincerity born of desperation.

"No, what is wrong with *you?*"

Lee massaged the back of her neck and stared at Taylor, exasperated. *Damn, I love this woman,* Lee thought, *everything about us hurts but I still fuckin love this woman.*

Taylor stood across the room, arms braided across chest, an ocean of distance between them.

"When are we—" Lee stopped, breathed in and started again in a calmer tone. "When are *we* gonna get to spend time together? You're always leaving to be with someone else."

"It's not like you sit at home waiting for me, and besides, I have the right to go out if I wanna go out," Taylor said.

"I know that. I just feel like ... you're avoiding dealing with me and our relationship."

Taylor slowly shrugged, tired and annoyed. "Maybe I am. Maybe I'm not ready."

"Why are you about to chill with Sy right now? Sy likes you and you *know* that."

"So?"

Lee's neck snapped back. "*So?* You don't think her wanting you matters?"

"Not really."

"What—"

Taylor put her hand up. "Sy does not like me like *that* and even if she did, she respects our relationship too much to do anything."

"Do *you* respect our relationship too much to do anything?"

Taylor smiled cynically. "What do you think?"

"I really don't know, that's why I'm asking. You keep pushing me away like you want to leave. *Do you* want to leave?"

"What does that mean?"

"Do you want to leave me?" Lee asked, an edge in her voice.

"Do you want to be left?" Taylor snapped back.

"We're going in circles, Taylor. Why are we talking in circles? What happened to us?"

"You know what the fuck happened."

"When ... how are we going to get back to the way we were?" Lee asked, concern coloring her voice.

"Never. It can never be like that because I'm not the same, you're not the same, everything changed the minute you ... did that."

"Are you fuckin her?"

Taylor laughed. "Sy?"

"Yes, Sy. Are you fuckin her? To punish me? Is that what the fuck you're doing?" Lee's voice rose. "I don't know why you can't forgive me. There are so many things I've forgiven you for—"

"*Please.* Like what? For loving you, for being there?"

"You're acting like a victim."

"Acting like a—" Taylor slammed her hands to her forehead and screamed in frustration. "What are you talking about? You *made* me a victim and now that's all I am!" Taylor turned her back to Lee.

"Taylor?" Taylor didn't move. "We have to work through this if we're gonna be together."

"No," Taylor said.

"No?" Lee repeated, almost choking on the word.

"Yes: *no.* It should *not* be that simple."

"What are you talking about?"

Taylor's back was still turned, her fingers interlocked and clasping the back of her neck. "I want you to feel what I felt. I can't just *work through it* like a math problem. It's not over."

"Baby—"

"Don't *baby* me. I'm fucking pissed off. 'I'm sorry' doesn't make it better. You won't ever understand till you're as helpless as I was."

"Don't you see ... it was *because* I felt helpless that I hurt you like that."

"Shut the fuck up, Lee, because I don't want to hear it!" Taylor spun around, screaming with an intensity that shocked and scared Lee. "I don't care about how *you* felt! What about *me?* What about how I felt, feel, *still feel right now?* I don't trust you. In our bed I'm lonely because I don't know when you'll feel the need to control me like that again and that's not love!"

"What the hell—" Lee dodged the books flying toward her except the one that hit her side.

"Shut up!" Taylor picked up a snow globe and threw it. Lee ducked, and it shattered against the wall behind her.

Taylor screamed, "I don't want to—*work!* You hurt me! You hurt me and now when you touch me, you fuckin disgust me!"

Taylor moved quickly across the room, closing the distance between them. "Taylor—"

"No."

Taylor slapped Lee's face.

Lee glared at her as if she was a stranger. She grabbed Taylor's shoulders. *Hard.*

Taylor inhaled sharply.

Shocked, Lee felt naked. Her armor of perpetual cool had been chiseled wide open and she had nowhere to hide and she knew Taylor saw the fear shining through. A tear crawled down Lee's cheek as she released Taylor's shoulders and backed away. Lee grudgingly licked her top lip where her tear had landed. Nostrils flared, Lee maintained eye contact as she backed toward the door.

There was no anger in Lee's eyes; just sadness.

When Lee opened the door, Sy was standing there. Lee walked past her without a word.

FOR SIZAKELE

forever is long

Nervous, I bit my inner cheek.

Over and over.

Over and over.

Sy and I stood in silence for a minute, immersed in the moment.

"Taylor . . . ?"

I looked around me at the books lying wide open across the room; the broken snow globe lay shattered on the floor, its glass edges menacing as shark teeth. My palm still tingled from the impact with Lee's face.

My voice was too shaky to be mistaken as normal. "So you ready to go?"

"Taylor, what the—"

"Let's go," I said.

Sy and I went to a bar close to campus. I said I wanted to get drunk but knew I couldn't, knew it wouldn't change anything but my coordination and judgment. I ordered a very non-alcoholic mango juice instead and sipped it, chewing on the occasional mango chunk.

"I think it's possible that I'm going crazy," I said.

"Taylor—"

"I really think it's possible that I'm going crazy."

I was calmer now, and could see Lee clearer in retrospect. Lee had been shook up and blown like I had never seen her.

Lee had opened up parts of herself to me that no one else had ever seen. When she felt relaxed and safe in my arms—*when* she was in my arms, which hadn't happened lately—she would share things with me so close to her heart, that all I could do was hold her tighter to show her how honored I was that she would share such things with me.

When I first met Lee, I'd loved her dedication to her

athleticism. I'd thought her devotion was sexy—no matter how late we were up making love the night before, she never missed her morning run. Lee's apartment was a testament to her dedication—her ever-present blue and gray gym bag, the weights around her apartment, and dirty sweats or basketball shorts tossed on top of her hamper. I was amazed at her ability to bust her ass weightlifting, cross-training, running, going to basketball practice, attending classes, then come home, sleep, get up at dawn and do it all over again. I never thought of it as anything more than a love of the game and a desire to stay in shape. Until three months ago, last Christmas.

❧

It was a few days before our holiday break last year. I had just put the finishing touches on my fifteen-page Comparative Lit paper. My paper compared and explored the lyricism of Chrystos with the anti-colonialist truth-telling of Ngũgĩ wa Thiong'o. I saw both as examples of protest literature—literature that contests, upsets and redefines an oppressive status quo. *Pure literary fierceness.*

"You bought your ticket home yet?" I asked absently, still engrossed in my laptop.

"I'm not going home," Lee had said. Clad in gray sweats, she sank into the couch, nudging off her sneakers heel to toe and pushing them under the coffee table.

"What? Why not?" I looked at her, surprised.

She brushed her hoodie off her head with a weary hand. "I don't want to talk about it."

"Lee, baby, how are you spending the holidays?"

"On campus. I'll just keep training."

"You're going to miss the holidays to *train?* Come on, you know that's not right," I'd said.

"I don't want to be home. I'd rather be anywhere besides home."

"Really?"

"Yes. When I left for college, I promised myself I would never go back. That's why I became an athlete."

"What do you mean?"

She'd seemed hesitant. But she had continued. "I needed a way out of that house. I didn't trust my parents to pay my tuition. My father was barely around and my mother … we don't get along. I knew I didn't want to have to get a full-time job *and* be a student at the same time, so I figured I'd be the best athlete I could and try to get a scholarship. Turns out being 5'11", having a perfect jump shot and being kind of obsessive about winning is worth something." I smiled. "So no, I'm not going home. Ever."

"You *never* wanna go home? For real?" I asked.

"For real."

"Forever is long, baby."

"Yes, it is." Lee balled up her fists and laid them on her knees.

"But why, Lee?"

She didn't say anything. "Baby, I wanna be there for you but I can't if I don't even know what's going on."

"I was raped when I was a kid."

"What?"

I felt my heart, discordant with confusion and rage, tumbling inside my ribcage. I set my laptop aside.

"I told my mother. She was the first person I told. I ran home crying to her. I was bloody—" her voice cracked. Lee cleared her throat and stared at the ceiling. "She didn't believe me." Her jaw muscles danced angrily, clenching and unclenching. "So she's dead to me."

I got up from my chair and joined her on the couch. "Baby … I'm so sorry. Is it okay if I touch you?"

"Why wouldn't it be okay?"

"Because of what we're talking about. I didn't wanna assume. I don't wanna do the wrong thing."

"It's fine."

I placed a hand on her belly. "Do you want to talk—"

"I never wanna talk about it." Lee was stoic. "I just didn't know how else to explain why I'm not going home for Christmas."

"You don't have to talk about it to me if you don't want to. But if you want to, I want to listen."

"I know I'm being weird—"

"You're not being weird." She looked over at me, skeptical. "You're not. Be however the fuck you wanna be."

Lee smiled a quarter of a smile and leaned her head against the couch, looking into my eyes. "I love you. You gully as shit."

"I love you too, King. You can come home to Vermont with me for the holidays. You know that, right?"

"No, I don't."

"You definitely can. My mom is a seriously good cook, and this way we don't have to miss each other," I said. "On New Year's Eve, we can watch the ball drop. It'll be fun."

Her smile was reluctant. "Okay. Okay. But I'm running five miles every morning."

"Yes, sir."

ଓଃ

Christmas morning, we'd gone sledding; we'd tumbled down the hill laughing so hard my sides had ached. I missed *that* us, the laughter of us.

"Taylor? Taylor? Hello?"

I blinked mad times and brought myself back to the present moment. "Sorry, Sy. I was *definitely* lost in a memory."

"You wanna talk about it?"

"No, not really."

Today I'd seen another part of Lee—a fear I had caused. I

saw threads of her composure and trust in me coming undone. Something in me had struck out at her in pain, in a frantic need to be powerful, to not have to feel helpless. A desperate part of me that was tired of hearing "sorry" had put her down like she'd held me down to try to control her and the situation.

Now, within the secrecy of my thoughts, I was looking for a reason, an excuse. So what if Lee's pissed me off, *who gives a fuck?* So what if Lee frustrates me and sometimes doesn't understand me? Sometimes *I* don't understand me, when did frustration give me the right to hit—

Maybe I hit you for hurting me, maybe it's the only way to pull you down to where you pushed me. But where are we now? Abusing each other to prove points?

Guilt twisted my heart and regret fluttered within me, wringing my stomach. I wanted to go see Lee but was scared she might not want to see me.

When I looked up from my drink, Sy was staring at me, worried.

"I'm gonna go home," I said.

"Are you sure that's what you want to do?"

"Yeah … and stop looking at me like that."

"I'll walk you."

"No, you won't, and please don't insist. I'll be fine."

"At least finish your drink." I gulped down the rest of my drink and we both got up. She hugged me tightly. "Call me if you need anything. It doesn't matter when."

"Thank you." I looked at her. Such a beautiful friend she'd become in such a short period of time. "Really—thank you, Sy."

After I left I didn't go home. I caught the 4 train at Union Square with no destination in mind. I rode the train for hours. I sat in a corner, staring unseeing at the walls of the train, not noticing who got on and off, not hearing the electronic voice announce each stop.

In those milliseconds before hitting her I had somehow

thought that I would feel powerful by striking back at her, but instead I felt small and ashamed—ashamed that I'd made myself a hypocrite, ashamed that I had become all I had accused her of being.

Where was my self-righteous anger *now?*

ꕥ

Even though I had a key, I knocked. I anxiously picked at my fingers as I waited for Lee to answer.

She didn't.

I let my fingertips travel across the surface of the wooden door then pressed my palms urgently into the door, trying impossibly to reach through and feel her.

"Lee." I sighed, feeling shitty and defeated. "I can understand why you wouldn't want to see me and you don't have to, but … I'm sorry. *I'm really sorry.*"

ꕥ

A few days later, I returned to Lee's, and found her leaning against her building.

I hesitated.

I'd anticipated having the time during my walk up three flights of stairs to breathe and get my mind right before seeing her. Instead, there she was, staring off somewhere so far away she didn't notice me walking up.

"I didn't know you smoked," I said, not knowing what else to say—even though there was so much to say.

All the familiarity was gone from Lee's face, like she had lost all memory of who I was. In a voice full of checked rage, she said, "I didn't know you were physically abusive."

Damn. I sighed, not knowing what to say after that. *I didn't know I was either.*

Lee shifted her weight, her tan Timberlands crunching

the snow into the concrete beneath her. "I'm sure you have brilliantly deconstructed why you hit me."

"I—"

"I'm sure you've been feeling sorry for yourself," Lee said.

"Lee …"

"Are you here with an updated list of what I've been doing wrong?"

"Lee, that's not how I think of you. I *love* you."

"Why didn't you say that when I needed to hear it?" Her eyes looked tired.

"I don't—"

"You don't *know.* You don't know anything, so why the fuck are you *here?*" she said, letting her anger rush full force into me.

"I know you need space and I can understand that—"

"You think I need space?" Lee sounded like she was joking, but nothing was funny.

"Yeah …"

"This is your idea of space, you up in my face feeling sorry for yourself?"

"I was hoping we could talk."

"*Now* you wanna talk about some shit," she snapped.

I was trying trying *trying* to be understanding, to be the evil yet forgiveness-worthy perpetrator who deserved to have my sentences interrupted, whose voice should be cautious/tentative/uncertain, who didn't have the right to have any strong opinions, but now I was *pissed* and I knew I would explode if I even halfway started talking about why. Wasn't it five minutes ago that I was being accused of cheating for no reason? And wasn't it fifteen minutes before that that I was held down in my own bed against my will? *Not to bring up old shit, but the shit ain't that fuckin old.*

"You know what Lee—how about I leave? Obviously you don't want to talk and I'm not gonna stand here and let you shit your rage all over me."

FOR SIZAKELE

breathe ma, breathe

"Sy."

I sighed.

Brooklyn's nighttime horizon filled her bedroom window. The sky was full of more lights than I could count and that comforted me somehow. I curled my yellow-socked feet under myself on top of Sy's covers, and leaned back against her wrought-iron headboard.

"You melt my anger like chocolate under fire," I said.

Sy laughed. "Are you serious? I didn't know people actually talked like that." She handed me a drink, then grabbed the magenta throw blanket from the foot of the bed and draped it around her body. She laid beside me on the bed.

"I didn't know I could actually feel like this."

Sy is very, very beautiful. There is a point where she stops being real sometimes because I can't really grasp why she is this beautiful. "You're good for me," I said softly. "Very, very good."

She seemed flattered and humbled in a way that I had never seen. "Odaro, you're good for me too."

"Really?"

"Yes. What—you're surprised?"

"I guess so. I just didn't think of our relationship in terms of me being good for you." I looked over at her. "You don't seem like you need anyone to be good to you."

She laughed, louder this time. "So I come off that big and bad?"

"Uh, *yeah,*" I said, teasing her. "You seem to have your shit together."

"That's good, because most of the time I don't feel that way."

"You are definitely good for me," I said. "Especially tonight when I need to be calmed down."

"I'm not gonna rush you to tell me about whatever it is that's bothering you, but you know you can whenever you're ready."

"I saw Lee with her ex today."

"Vraiment?"

"Yeah, she was getting into Lee's car."

"Don't let yourself assume anything," she cautioned.

"Assume anything? What's there to assume? My girlfriend and her ex-girlfriend, getting into a car to go somewhere together. I'm not assuming anything. I'm not assuming she still loves me, not assuming she still wants me in her life—"

"Taylor, you can't torture yourself like this, especially when you don't have all the facts. Maybe they were just going to lunch or something?"

"After a year of them not speaking to each other, and after we've been dealing with mad shit these past three months, *now* they're meeting up and hugged up in the parking lot?" I rolled my eyes. "May I have another drink, please?"

"Bien sûr. What you want?"

"Can I get a White Russian? But isn't that a little re-re-re—what the fuck is that word?"

"*Re-re-reeeeee*gurgitate all the food in your stomach if you keep drinking!"

"Shut up! Redundant. Isn't White Russian redundant, since all Russians are white?" I started to laugh hysterically. "Laugh wan kill me dead!"

"There's got to be Black Russians. Black people are *everywhere,*" she said. Sy laughed so hard that she could barely mix my drink.

"You're supposed to be my bartender!" I said. "How's the bartender gonna be so fucked up she can't pour my drink?"

"Abeg! Maybe if you tipped me better, I'd try harder to stay sober for you!"

We lost our breath to our laughter; everything was the funniest shit we had ever seen or heard, no matter how tiny or simple or everyday or stupid. I made fun of the hearts on her blanket, then laughed at her defense that her grandma had knit it for her and that she hadn't had the "heart" to tell her that at 21 years old, hearts and flowers were cute but not as sophisticated as she was trying to be. Imagining that conversation had me laughing until I was speechless.

Later, after maybe our 63rd fit of giggles, we were breathing deeply, our bellies still aching, but quiet within a happy little piece of peace. She reached across her bed to lay her hand on top of mine. "It'll be okay."

I looked into her eyes and it was different from the hundreds of other times I'd looked into her eyes. This time I didn't hold back the sensuality I felt. Maybe it was the liquor. Maybe it was seeing Ahsha and Lee together. I felt bold. *No, not bold … true.* I felt like *myself,* without any bullshit or worries. My whole body felt like a verse written stream of consciousness, uncensored words feverishly crashing out of the tip of my pen without apology. This moment was a pure perfect poetic something. Distilled and unedited.

I put my other hand on top of hers.

I knew she knew what I meant.

I started to think but stopped myself. I started to chastise myself but stopped. I cut off the lectures forming in my head.

I didn't want to think or analyze or realize that at that moment what I seriously wanted was to cheat on my girlfriend.

I could tell she was going to speak because the syllables started forming alliances in her eyes, so I was ready with my "Don't" when she said: "Taylor—"

"But—"

"Please. *Don't.*"

And she was quiet for me.

A little later, I couldn't resist asking. "What is this?"

"What is what?"

"This between us."

"Taylor, I think we're on our way to being drunk."

"No, *this,*" I said, and I squeezed her hand to let her know what I meant. "This feels …" I closed my eyes and felt a little dizzy. "… sweet." We sat, hands touching, souls glowing, hearts showing. We were innocent; no bad history, no baggage, no garbage, just … *sweet.* "I need this."

"Taylor …" she said all breathy, and I had to smile.

"It's not the White Russians speaking for me," I said. "You're just beautiful."

"I know," she said, all smart-ass and bad-ass, and we laughed.

And then we were quiet again.

ଓଃଌ

I wanted Sy to hold me, to wrap her arms around me and *hold me.*

She did.

She let me breathe. Breath after breath came up out of me like an avalanche of air and I breathed deeply like I had needed to for months, maybe years. As we lay, she said softly, "*You* soothe *me*, Taylor."

I didn't believe her.

"How?"

"Your sweetness, your incredibly big heart, how vulnerable you are, how caring and loving," she said. "Everything about you is beautiful."

"Wow. I didn't know you thought about me like that."

"Of course. How else is there to think about you?"

I smiled. "Girl, your game is tight."

"No game. Seulement la vérité."

Maybe Lee was right about Sy and me. Maybe every dinner and every secret part of ourselves Sy and I had shared with each other over the past few months was a prelude to this: lying in her arms, *sensual thoughts drifting through my mind that I really didn't mind.* Yes, it mattered that Lee might be having sex with her ex, but then again, it really *didn't* matter, and that wasn't why I was there. I *wanted* to be lying in Sy's bed. It was so easy to be with her, so *unbelievably easy* to laugh and sleep and talk and be. I just wanted to be, and be easy for once.

The little lines we drew around our relationships began to blur. I mean, do friends hold each other like this … or like *this?* Am I allowed to think about her lips? Am I allowed to lay my head on her shoulder? Yes? What about right in the crook of her neck, my cheek pressed into the curve of her neck? Is that okay? Or can only lovers' bodies be this close? Are we flirting now? Or being good friends to each other? Platonic, romantic; what's symptomatic of what? Of the millions of ways there are to be intimate, we chose the ones that blurred the lines.

I rolled onto my side, facing her. *This is why I don't drink.* Because when I'm sober I can easily keep all my inappropriate feelings in check. My eyes lingered on her lips longer than necessary, then flickered up to her eyes.

"I want to touch you," I said, with a simplicity that surprised me. "Right here." I placed my hand on the smooth sliver of skin exposed between the edge of her tank top and her jeans.

"This is not the time—" Sy began.

"Not the time for what?"

"Not the time to try to distract yourself from the pain you're feeling by flirting with me."

"You think you're a distraction?"

"Yes I do." Sy looked at me seriously. "I *won't* be your dis—"

"Syrus, I want to *touch* you. I have wanted to touch you for a long time. I'm just finally admitting it."

"We're drunk."

"Queen, I am *tipsy,* not so drunk I can't make choices I'll stand by in the morning. But if you are …" I pulled my hand away. Sy watched me place my hand on the bed between us. She grabbed me from low on the back of my waist and swiftly, smoothly pulled me to her. Our breath danced together, our noses almost touching.

"I'm not drunk," Sy said. We had never been this close, not like this. "But let's sleep off the tipsy. If we still want to … whatever when we wake up, then maybe we can … whatever."

"Okay." We snuggled into each other's warmth.

A few hours later, I woke up beside Sy, feeling the rise and fall of her breathing and the heat of her body. Our breasts and bellies and pussies were kissing each other through our clothes, even in our sleep. Sy's hand was firm at the base of my spine, deliberate, strong, tender.

"Je veux te toucher comme le ciel ne horizon. Toujours," she said.

"Ça veut dire quoi? Wait, maybe I can figure it out … I want to touch you—"

"Like sky …"

"Does horizon."

"Oui." Her voice resonated with affection. "'I want to touch you like sky does horizon. Always.'" Sy's gaze felt like a sultry caress. "That's from one of my favorite French poems."

Her hand went up the inside of the back of my shirt, slow and warm. I wanted to moan her name. I smiled.

"Why the smile?"

"I feel shy."

"Why shy?"

"Your hand … your hand is making me want to moan."

"Then moan," she said.

As her hand worked its way up my back, I let breath escape my mouth, the slightest of sounds coming from my throat. My hand slid over the curve of her hip onto her behind; I looked into her dark eyes and moved my lips closer to hers. My breath was rising and falling in waves as Sy's hand traveled over my belly button and *up up up*, one finger caressing the curve of the bottom of my breast. I moaned her name and she smiled. How could she make me this wet with just one touch and innuendo? I kissed her smile, and the softness of her lips made me press my body into hers, grab her behind firmly and then we were pulling each other, pushing into each other, breathing loud, biting lips. *I wanted to burst out of my skin and clothes into her body.* When I pushed my thigh between her thighs, Sy pulled away, her hand on my thigh tenderly halting my progression, her eyes murmuring sweet things to me, her wet lips pink and swollen.

"We have to stop." She placed one last kiss on my lips; I knew it was the last one from the way she lingered. Hearts thumping in our chests and without words, we knew if my thigh ran into her pussy our clothes would evaporate.

଼

"I miss the snow," I said to Sy's bedroom ceiling a few hours later.

"Really?" Sy asked.

"Yeah. I spent my childhood in Vermont, so to me snow is like air. I'm used to feet upon feet of snow, not just a light dusting."

"Winter is still a foreign thing to me …" Sy's voice trailed off.

I found Sy's eyes. In the pictures playing across her pupils, there was an image I recognized. Sometimes I would find Sy lost in thought and many of those times there was a distance I couldn't cross and never tried to. This time, though, I saw a strange intensity in her eyes I'd never seen before. My eyes searched hers, looking for something elusive.

"I'm sorry ma, what were you saying?" Sy shook her head lightly, coming back from far away. The images vacated her eyes like a television screen gone blank. I kept looking at her until she asked, "What?"

"Madiko, where did you go?"

"What?"

"Or should I ask … what's her name?"

"Who?"

"That woman you just went to."

"I was just a little distracted for a second."

Distracted would be an understatement; it was like her being was subtracted from her body and living within a memory for those few seconds. Sy had gone to a different time.

"Where were you?"

"Nowhere. Now what were you saying?"

"Nothing. You were talking and then you stopped," I said. "Is it easier to fix all the fractured parts of me than to talk about what's going on with you?"

"It's not that deep."

"So you're not going to tell me?"

She lowered her eyes.

"Sy, I can see you're in pain—"

"How do you know I'm in pain?"

"Because of your eyes."

"What about my eyes?"

"There's this combination of hurt and regret … the kind that takes a long time to build."

Sy looked self-conscious. "Am I that transparent?"

"No, I'm that observant. You know everything about me except my fuckin social security number. I would love it if you'd let me be there for you in the way you always are for me."

Silence. Sy looked like a thoughtful kind of sad.

"We lived together. In this apartment. She bought those dishes I put your dinner on." Sy shook her head ever so slightly. "We fought a lot, too damn much. In the beginning, before the fighting, we used to dance and sing all the time. Toward the end, we stopped dancing, stopped singing … Sometimes I think I loved her a little too much, and not enough at the same time."

"How is that possible?"

"I don't know. But it feels like I loved her too much if I still feel this way two years after she left. Not enough … because she left me, Taylor." She looked into my eyes with an honesty that made my heart ache. "I wonder if I didn't give her enough of the love she wanted, how she wanted it. She used to say I was trying to change her. She would scream it at me. Maybe she was right."

"Madiko ..."

"Her name was ... her name *is* Elle."

imprint

She's more than. Elle is much more than the one that got away, she is the one, the only one. The one I can't let go of, want back, who shook my spirit, who drove me to utter confusion, and from confusion to clarity. She was the sexiest woman ever and her touches were heavy. Her touches were so heavy, the day she left me, she placed a finger on my lips/the imprint of which/I still feel today. I don't talk about her; I have these long winding thoughts that I think to her, and I propel my thoughts to her hoping she propels herself back to me.

I sing to her. Sometimes I feel her hearing me. I sing her the French songs my mama taught me. Mon amour, reviens-moi.

FOR SIZAKELE

cell block

All my tongue could taste was fried plantain, the crispy brown edges hot from the frying pan, with cold coconut ice cream melting on top. My craving drove me to the nearest bodega a few blocks from my dorm. Well … I headed for the nearest bougie little bodega-*esque* corner market, fully aware that I would probably pay a good 30% more for my cravings than I would in Harlem, Brooklyn, Queens or the Bronx. In white wide-leg pants, a yellow tank top and a sea-green wrappa wrapped around my shoulders and torso, I marveled at the warmth of spring and how brisk the air felt. I wanted to cook in my mama's kitchen but would have to settle for frying up this deliciousness in my dorm's common kitchen. My phone rang as I entered the bodega, and I smiled at the name on my screen. "A.C.! What a beautiful surprise to hear from you!"

"I've been thinking about you," A.C. said. "I hadn't heard back from you since my last email and wanted to check on you. How are you?"

Lee and me.

Our beautiful, fucked up ugliness.

"Oghene?" she asked.

"Yeah?"

"How you dey?"

"Heartbroken."

"Love …"

"My heart aches every day. I'm with a woman I don't trust anymore." I paused and looked down the bodega aisle to make sure no one was within earshot. "A.C., she came so close to raping me. And there wasn't a fuckin thing I could've done to stop her."

"Chineke Fadda God! Have you talked to anyone about this?"

"Yes."

"What happened?"

I wandered down aisles in search of ice cream but got distracted by all the different kinds of everything. Rice noodles, soba noodles … lemon soy sauce, tamarind chutney—

"Taylor, you there?"

"Yeah, yeah. Sorry. I'm at the bodega and got a little distracted. Um, I told you a little bit about this in my email. So … a couple months back, I came home and she must have been waiting for me because she knocked on my door two seconds after I got home. She was mad because she couldn't reach me all day and because I was having dinner with a friend. We started kissing and then were on the bed … but it never felt like that before, so rough and … strange. She was like another person. We've had rough sex before but it was *never* like that, it was *always* consensual and we'd *always* stop whenever either of us said stop. This time she didn't. She pinned my hands above my head … and was grabbing me … with so much *anger.* She was so rough. She put her hand around my throat and I could barely breathe." I breathed deeply to calm myself. "After she got off me, we started fighting, and she called me Chris."

"Chris? Who's Chris?"

"Her cousin. He raped her when she was 13."

"Na wa. Why would she call you by his name?"

"I don't know."

"Has she ever done that before?"

"No, never."

"Do you think she really thought you were him? Was it a Freudian slip of tongue or did she actually stop seeing you and start seeing him?"

My eyes wandered over the plethora of food items but I didn't see any of them. "I don't know what she thinks or who she saw. She hasn't brought up calling me his name. She apologized for everything *except* that. I'm kinda scared to go there. On the rare occasion that she talks about the rape, I try to be supportive of her, but it's so hard, A.C. It makes me feel so helpless to watch what she's going through and it's stressful, to say the least, to talk about Chris or her sexual assault. I'm still angry about what she did to me, I don't know if I have the strength to go there right now and talk about *her* pain and why she called me his name. Do you understand what I mean?"

"Of course I do. You don't know if you can support her when she hurt you, and you're still hurting. You're not her therapist, you know that, right? As her girlfriend, of course you will support her, but she has to take care of herself emotionally and get the help she needs from people besides you." A.C. paused. "I'm so sorry she was violent toward you. Maybe she hurt you because she can't hurt him?"

"How can she even make that connection? It's not my fault she was raped—"

"I know, I know, and I'm *not* saying it is. It's just when you're a survivor of sexual assault, it takes so much emotional and spiritual work to be able to have a healthy sex life, and I don't know if she's done the work it takes." A.C.'s voice was soothing. "It's a constant, lifelong process of healing. I know she must be dealing with a lot of pain, but her pain does not justify her turning around and causing you pain. Are you getting the support you need? What do *you* need right now?"

"To escape my life, to run away. I need a fuckin break." I contemplated whether I wanted mango-lime jam or kale chips. Corn chips. Rice crisps? *Ten dollars for jam, though?*

"A vacation, nko?" A.C. suggested.

"Yes o. A vacation would be amazing right about now."

"You're welcome to come to Oakland any time, and of course you can stay at my crib."

Her generosity made me want to cry. "Thank you, A.C. Maybe in the summer. Right now I have classes, exams, my jobs, blah blah blah. I can't just leave … even though I really want to."

"Are you gonna stay with—what's your girlfriend's name?"

"Lee."

"Are you gonna stay with Lee?"

"I don't know."

"That's some serious shit, Taylor. Obviously you love her, and that's why you're with her, but you have to love yourself, too."

"Right now, I feel like my love for Lee is an unfortunate fact I can't escape."

"You know I teach poetry in prisons four days a week, right?"

"I remember you telling me that, yeah." I spotted some plantain in a cardboard box on the ground. I picked through the green and green-yellow ones until I found the ripe yellow ones. I grabbed two.

"These women are brilliant. Most of them got caught up in a fucked up situation, and then in an even more fucked up judicial system that doesn't give a fuck about their bruises or the daily terror they suffered before they snapped and killed the bastard who was raping them on the daily." A.C. paused a moment, then continued. "I say this not to be morbid or pessimistic but to add another perspective. Most women in prison are there for nonviolent crimes, but of the ones who were convicted of violent crimes, many of them are there for defending themselves or their babies against violence, usually from a partner. Because that's my work, my mind is always there. I just want you to be careful and try to make sure the violence doesn't escalate."

"You think she'd hurt me?"

"Sweetheart, she's *already* hurt you."

"I mean so bad that the police would have to be called?"

"I don't know. Whether olokpa dey, I think that violence is more likely to happen between unhappy, emotionally repressed partners. I'm just sayin, Oghene. If Lee could strangle you, who knows what else she could do? And then who knows what you might have to do to protect your neck?"

"But—"

"But what? But you love her? She loves you? She didn't mean it? She's just stressed right now? Things will change? You deserved it? Don't go there, *please don't go there.* The word 'love' don't mean a thing. It's what you *do* that means something. Love is a verb, right?"

I leaned against the end of an aisle and stared at the tiles near my feet. I didn't want to feel all the feelings that were tumbling and climbing to the surface because of A.C.'s candid, loving words. Tears were en route to my eyes and I wanted my eyes to swallow them back. *I don't have the time or energy to feel this shit.* So I focused on the tiles.

"Oghene?"

"Yeah?"

"I'm sorry."

"For what?"

"I'm sorry for switching into counselor-advocate mode. I don't mean to tell you what to do. That's not why I called. I called to check on you, as a friend."

I didn't say a word.

"You mad?"

"No," I said, my voice shaking.

"You are, I knew it. Shit, I'm sorry. I just got so protective of you—"

I took a deep breath to steady myself. "I get that you're concerned and that means a lot to me. I just ... don't want to be lectured."

"I didn't mean it that way, I'm sorry. I'm just worried about you."

"I know." I made myself move from where I'd been leaning and proceeded toward the ice cream section. "I'm also just ... trying not to cry, trying not to feel this enough to hurt enough to cry and then fall apart and not be able to get out of bed. I'm exhausted with all the feeling I'm capable of. Sometimes I just want to be one of those insensitive fucks who go through life feeling one-tenth of what I feel. I don't talk about my relationship—co-dependent, abusive, whatever-the-fuck we are—because I can't deal with this shit, I just can't."

I opened the sliding door and fingered the possibilities. Soy coconut ... pineapple coconut ... I grabbed the chai coconut ice cream.

"You're a beautiful—"

"Really? If I'm so beautiful then why would Lee treat me the way she has? Why would you treat beauty that way?"

"How she treats you is not a measure of who you are. Just because you treat her like a king doesn't mean she deserves it. We are who we are regardless of how the people around us treat us."

I could no longer control my tears. "I wanna go home," I said.

"Where are you?"

"No, I mean home-home, to Naija. Sometimes I think everything would be better if I were home."

"I don't know about better, but definitely *hotter.*"

I laughed and wiped away my tears. "You're silly!" I made my way to the counter and paid for my food.

"Well I got you to laugh. That's good, right?" I mouthed "thank you" to the cashier and headed out the door.

"Yes, that's good. Whenever my heart hurts, I just wanna go home. The sun is different back home."

Naija sun is hot.

Thick like fufu.

An inescapable embrace I never want to leave.

"I know my parents had me here so I could have opportunity, education and all that good shit," I continued. "But I just miss my homeland. Nigerian food for every meal instead of on a special occasion at restaurant."

"I know, I know. *I know,*" A.C. said. "Oakland is fly, but it ain't Naija. I'm really sorry you're going through this."

"Me too, A.C. Me too."

FOR SIZAKELE

demerit system

Pacific Street was a moving photograph framed by Lee's living room window. I sat on the window ledge, my back to the street, oblivious to the hustle, the music, the movements below.

"I saw you with your ex last week!" I yelled so she could hear me in the bedroom. I waited for her to explain.

"Aren't you going to say anything?" I yelled again.

Lee stood in the bedroom doorway. "I was waiting for you to accuse me of something," she said.

"Lee, what do you expect me to think? Are you just gonna say nothing like it was perfectly innocent?"

"I wouldn't say it was 'perfectly innocent.'"

"What?"

"No one and nothing is ever really 'perfectly innocent,'" she explained.

"You think it's okay to be kickin it with your ex-girlfriend when we're having problems?"

"Look, it's not that serious, I was just giving her a ride—"

"She has her own car—"

"Which broke down."

"Where'd you give her a ride to?"

"Home."

"Here?"

"No, to her house."

"Did you stay?"

Lee rolled her eyes. "Yes."

"And did what?"

"You tight?" Lee leaned against the doorjamb and folded her arms across her chest, amused.

"What you expect? *Of course* I'm fuckin tight. *What did the two of you do?*"

"We talked."

"Why would you need to talk to your ex?"

"I don't know, Taylor, maybe I needed to talk to someone who had more positive than negative things to say about me, someone who wasn't hanging my mistakes over my head, someone who I could chill with, not be on edge with. I guess you could say she was my Sy for a day."

Damn. I had no witty retort for that.

"So she gives you something I can't?" I asked.

"You can cut that jealous shit out Taylor, *really,* because I'm not buying it."

"What's that supposed to mean? You don't believe I'm jealous?"

"No, I don't. You're not jealous. You're convinced of whatever you think you saw and whatever story you have in your head. No matter what I say, you're gonna think what you're gonna think, so why should I bother with the truth?"

"Can you tell me what happened without being sarcastic?"

"On that sarcasm tip, *obviously* I learned from the best. You've probably been fuckin Sy for who knows how long, so I don't know why you're so heated about what I'm doing."

"I am not fuckin Sy! How would you feel if you saw me with Nia?"

"Have you seen your ex lately?" Lee asked.

"No—"

"Then what's the point of a random hypothetical?"

"Because that seems to be the only way to get you to see my perspective. You know you were wrong to be chillin with Ahsha like that, especially when she's said over and over that she wants you back—"

"Are you gonna give me a fuckin demerit because of it? Mark it down next to the others. I'm out."

I rushed to physically block her from leaving. Resisting my natural urge to touch her, I asked: "Can we talk?"

She stared down at me blankly. "No."

Lee walked closer to the door. "Lee?" She paused and

raised her left eyebrow expectantly. "I, uh … I kissed Sy," I said. I braced myself against Lee's anger, but she didn't react.

"Of course you did. When?"

"Last week."

"For the first time?" she asked.

"Yes."

"What took you so long?"

Lee walked out, the breeze from the shutting door a strange caress.

hammer

Lee headed into the music conservatory and went to her usual room.

Sat down at the shiny, black grand piano.

Let her backpack fall to the side of the bench, propped her left elbow on top of the piano.

She started playing a mash-up of Otis Redding's "That's How Strong My Love Is" and Teddy Pendergrass' "Come Go With Me." One-handed.

Her gray NYU hoodie framed her face and hung loose around her head. She started riffing:

"… you should know better,
yes, you
should *knooow* better,
your love like a mack truck
running over my bones.
you
should know better.
you
should know better."

The piano was still her best friend. Still the only place she completely relaxed and felt she could come undone. Lee's fingers caressed the keys with feather-light tenderness, then slammed down with intensity akin to anger.

Playing the piano always made Lee think of lovemaking, because of the dexterity required in both. Each touch has a reaction that resonates throughout an entire instrument, creating a world of sound. It made her happy to know that she could create such a world.

Lee remembered the first girl she'd made love to. They'd

both been in high school and she hadn't believed Lee was a virgin. She smiled a small smile remembering; it was all those years of faithful piano playing. Lee's first lover was also the first person to call her butch. She'd never known she was butch until people called her that; she knew that wasn't the name of her soul, but she had a love for the roughness of the word.

Butch.

So blunt. The word made no apologies for itself; there was no escaping its fullness.

"... I am
making love to
the brick wall
of you ..."

The piano was still how she felt close to her grandmother. She remembered sitting at the kitchen table as Nana baked chocolate chip cookies, strawberry rhubarb pie, banana bread and a million other delicious desserts. Her grandmother's baking kept that one-story Boston home warm in those brick winters.

Lee would sit at the round kitchen table, eyes beaming love at her grandmother, who vigorously whisked sweet batters and rolled out piecrusts made from scratch. Her grandmother's stories were the soundtrack that played as she baked. Lee would listen to Nana tell her how she used to go swing dancing in the 1940s in Harlem and Lee would smile, imagining the bright-colored dresses, the whirling skirts, the walls sweating and the live band jamming.

One spring day, air full of pollen and trees beginning to bloom, Lee hid in her grandmother's arms. She had run into those arms and stammered unintelligible half-sentences about Chris; her clothes were ripped, she had dirt on her face, and her private parts, elbows and knees were raw and bleeding. Her grandmother had listened and kept her face calm. When her mother had come around looking for Lee hours later, her grandmother had stood in the open doorway between them, a mountain of armor against her mother's disbelief.

"Listen here. LeAnna came here because she feels safe in this house—"

"Mama, that child is telling stories—"

"No child has a mind to make up a story that ugly. What kind of mother did I raise you to be that you don't believe your own child?"

"Why don't you believe *me,* mama?" Lee's mother protested.

"This child ain't had as much time on this earth to learn to be as cold as you. She ain't lying. And I'm not lettin her back into your house until you believe her."

She'd shut the door and turned to Lee. "Come here, baby."

Her grandmother taught her to play the piano, had told her, "Sometimes the only way to move on is to fill your heart with music. It's the only thing that saved me after your grandfather died." Her grandmother taught her about the piano from the inside out, and Lee had always been fascinated by the hammer, the part that connected the keys with the strings inside the piano, creating a ricochet domino effect that made the music possible.

Her Nana had given her music, and music had held her and taken care of her ever since. At that moment, Lee wanted to call her grandmother so bad, wanted to talk to her about her life, about Taylor and what had happened, but she didn't know where to start or what to say. Tears tickled the backs of her eyes. For months, Lee felt like everything she did was one long apology for hurting Taylor. Who the fuck was she becoming that she could even strangle her in the first place? Taylor had been pushing her away for months now. That's what had brought her to the piano; she was feeling lost and lonely. And confused and disgusted at who she was turning into. Losing Taylor felt inevitable.

"you are
loving me
in the past tense"

Taylor didn't know half the shit she'd been through during her childhood. Lee left home with a promise to never return, and she hadn't. Not once. Not for birthdays or holidays or summers. New York was her home now. She didn't want to live in the same city as Chris or her mother and so she made a contract with basketball, a business deal: Lee would give everything to basketball and basketball would take her out of Boston and put her through college. Her grandmother was the only part of Boston she missed. And she missed her fiercely.

Opening up to Taylor had been a very slow process. Lee had been vague about her past on purpose, but loving Tay had made her inch open her heart bit by bit. Now Taylor was the one who was shut down emotionally—Taylor had turned into ... a hard butch who didn't talk about her feelings, who was out of bed before cuddling could happen, who fucked Lee with her clothes on.

Lee wanted to believe she could relax and let someone see her messy, fucked up past; see the abandonment by her mother, see the life she'd run far and fast from to save herself, see the pain in her chest that couldn't be soothed. But Lee couldn't let anyone see those parts of herself when she barely acknowledged them to herself. She tried to tell Taylor about the hard parts, but the words wouldn't come, and she was convinced Tay would think it was her fault or she wouldn't understand or she'd think Lee should just forgive her mother and make peace with her. Lee didn't want to hear any of that shit, so she didn't risk it.

"there are some things
I will never say to you
but I was hoping
one day
you'd ask"

If Sy and Taylor were fucking, what would she do? What really *could* she do? She remembered the beginning. Before their lives had grown so far apart. Lee was still hopeful that she could find the right words to coax Taylor to open up to her again; that if she was patient with Taylor's anger long enough, things could change. What hurt Lee the most about Taylor and Sy was not the possibility of them having passionate sex or sharing secrets; really, the hardest thing was seeing how Taylor's eyes sparkled when she spoke about Sy or their time together. Lee hadn't had a reaction when Tay told her about kissing Sy, because that wasn't the important thing to her. What *was* important was that spark in her eyes when she said Sy's name. That spark made Lee feel like she'd lost her already and there was nothing she could fuckin do about it.

ঔ

Lee left the conservatory at dusk and headed to the library to check out some books, melodies still tickling her mind. She looked a few titles up online to find the proper call number; wrote the call numbers onto a piece of paper, then took the elevator to the stacks on the third floor to grab the books. She turned down an aisle, looked up from the sheet of paper in her hand and saw Sy walking toward her.

"Hi," Sy said.

"Hi."

"Clearly this is awkward," Sy said hesitantly, her hands in the back pockets of her jeans.

"It's awkward because you're in love with my girlfriend."

"Okay, um, it seems we have a misunderstanding—"

"What's there to misunderstand? Didn't you and Taylor kiss?"

Sy gripped the back of her neck. "Um, yeah. We did."

"You know she's in a relationship with me, right?"

"Yes, I do, of course I do."

"So why the fuck are you kissing her?" Irritated, Lee clenched her jaw. Her nostrils flared.

"I don't think you should be talking with me about this."

"I think I should be talking to *exactly* you."

"Fine. Well, Lee, she kissed me too," Sy said.

Lee crossed her arms. "Does that make your actions okay? She kissed you too, so all bets are off?"

"No—"

"You need to walk away. She has me. If she wants to leave me for you, that's her choice. But she hasn't."

"It's up to Taylor to choose if she wants to spend her time with me," Sy said.

"Yes ... but no, it's up to all parties involved to act like grownups rather than pass the buck. How would you feel if you were me?"

Sy paused, then said quietly, "I'd ... I'd feel ... shitty."

"So why would you do something to someone else that you wouldn't want done to you?"

"It's not that simple."

"It *is* that simple. You're making it complicated so you can have an excuse to feel up my girlfriend." Lee raised her voice.

"Lee—"

"Keep my name *out* your mouth and stay away from Taylor."

"You treat her like shit, then act the role of the possessive, long-suffering girlfriend." Sy accused her with a tentative determination.

"It's not a *role,* this is my fuckin life. You don't know how I treat Taylor."

"I know what she tells me." Sy's palm found her chest and rested there, as if to comfort herself.

"Ohh, okay. So you get half the story and think you're an expert on a relationship you're not even *in?* Who the *fuck* are you to judge me? I could look at your behavior and call you a ho, but I'm sure there's more to you than this fucked up behavior you're exhibiting right now."

"I'm—"

"Look." Lee breathed deeply, attempting to calm down. "You need to fall back. *Hard.* If you don't like me or that we're together, *I don't really give a shit.* But you need to respect that we're together and back off. *Period.*"

Lee turned around and left without getting the books she needed.

watah don pass garri

The desk in my dorm room sat underneath a window that overlooked East 7th Street. I looked across the street at a large brick building; looked a little higher up and saw the blue spring sky. Opening my laptop, I smiled when I saw A.C. was online. I sent her an instant message.

Taylor: how you dey?
A.C.: i dey ooooo. good to hear from you. how bodi?
Taylor: bodi dey inside cloth. watah don pass garri, sef.
A.C.: sisí èkó, sorry o. how is your heart?
Taylor: this wahala dey break my heart o.
A.C.: if i was closer, i'd come over & cook for you.
Taylor: you cook?
A.C.: of course. suya is my specialty.
Taylor: don't torture me! unless you plan to overnight mail that deliciousness to me, i don't wanna hear it.
A.C.: lool. sorry o. tell me about this heartbreak wahala.
Taylor: *sigh* well, lee and i had this huge talk the other day. wait—did i tell you about sy? okay, let me back up. at first (after lee held me down) i felt mad angry. angry all the time. it started to crystallize into bitterness. and i was always short—short tempered, short sentences—i barely talked to lee. now i feel numb. in the midst of all this, i'm thankful for a new friend i've made, sy—

she's someone i can talk to about what's up with me. i feel at ease with her.

A.C.: re: sy—that's hella dope. re: numbness & anger—that's really hard. but it makes sense. you went through this really hard thing and your heart is trying to heal, because that's what we naturally do whether we know it or not. but the process is hard.

Taylor: this right here, what i'm going through definitely does not feel like healing. somewhere in me, i'm still in shock. like how could she do that to me?

A.C.: i don't know. it's not fuckin fair. but she is a survivor of horrendous abuse—

Taylor: so that makes it okay?? she went thru some mad hard shit so whatever bullshit she does is cool?

A.C.: NO. i am not saying that AT ALL.

Taylor: sorry, sorry. i know yr not. it just feels like i hv to be this perpetually understanding person and i don't have the fuckin strength for it.

A.C.: you don't have to be understanding or strong all the time, i'm not sayin that @ all. i bring up her past to give context, not make excuses. she was hurt really bad. i imagine she's still healing & she might not even know or see how what she survived affects you & yr relationship. i really hope you're not blaming yourself. her relationship to chris is complicated. he's family *and* her perpetrator. maybe her lashing out @ you is part of her dealing with her rage from what he did? that's what i'm trying to say.

Taylor: maybe. i try to support her. she

has nightmares and i hold her. i suggested therapy and she shut that suggestion down. i try to bring chris up, she leaves the apt instead of talking about it. i can't make her choose to heal or process it.

A.C.: wetin you go do? you go carry her pain for your head? you supporting her does not mean you create or micromanage her healing process. she has to take the lead & define it, not you. maybe she's not ready. or maybe her healing doesn't look how you'd expect. either way, how she's treated you is not your fault.

Taylor: it feels like it is. maybe it's not my fault… but i feel the weight of it so strong.

A.C.: that's not fair.

Taylor: that's my day to day. i barely recognize myself—i'm so angry.

A.C.: are you taking care of yourself?

Taylor: not really. well … sometimes. i don't know.

A.C.: you have to be easy on yourself. take some time to just do silly shit sometimes. it'll take time to figure everything out. for lee to figure things out & for you, too.

Taylor: you're right, bros. it's just … hard.

A.C.: I know. never hesitate to reach out to me. Oghene, I'm sorry but I have to head to work. make I come carry go. talk later, abi?

Taylor: abi. thank you.

A.C.: anytime o. xo.

crowded eyes

"Hello?" I mumbled into the phone.

"Desolée. Did I wake you?"

"Oh nono," I said, stifling a yawn. "Sy?"

"Oui. You sure I didn't wake you?"

"Well … I was just sneaking a little nap in, but go ahead, talk to me. I've been meaning to call you."

"Taylor, you were never gonna call me."

"No, really—" then I realized she was fuckin with me. "It's mean to harass people who are half-asleep and can't totally defend themselves," I said groggily, then started to laugh. "Sy! Seriously, I … I really wanted to call you to talk about the other day."

"That's what I'm calling you about, too. I wanted to thank you."

"Thank me? For what? I'm the one who keeps emotionally draining you."

"Oh, right, like I didn't take you on a little roller coaster when I emotionally left the building when I was thinking about Elle? I need to thank you, I mean *really* thank you for pushing me to open up about her. I've deliberately not dealt with those feelings and it means a lot that you cared enough to keep at me until I talked about it, even if it was only for a little bit."

"Any time. It seems like you're really hurting over her."

"I am," she said in a small voice. "I don't know when it will stop."

"You wanna talk about it?"

"I don't know what to say, Taylor. It's been two years and I still miss her. Maybe that's stupid of me."

"That is *not* stupid of you. Have you ever thought about calling her?"

"She changed her number and I don't know where she is."

"Damn."

"Yeah. I know I could get her number if I really wanted to. I know people close to her who I could ask for it … but I just can't bring myself to do that." Sy sucked her teeth. "Abeg, is it by force?"

"If you need to talk to her, you need to talk to her."

"That's true. Maybe it's my pride or my sense of what's right and wrong, but I know if she wanted me to know where she is, I would know. The fact that she changed her number makes me feel like she doesn't want me to reach her."

"There are a million reasons why people change their number, Sy; you can't assume the absolute worst reason. If you still love her and feel like you have to talk to her, then you need to get over your pride and face her."

Sy was quiet on the other side of the phone. "You're a really good friend."

"Madiko, you're an *amazing* friend. *I* should be thanking *you;* you've been so supportive and sweet." I exhaled softly, finding the courage to *just say it.* "And … I don't know how to talk about what happened between us the other day."

"You mean how we reached out to each other as friends and got sensual in how we comforted each other?"

"Yeah, that. How did you sum that all up in one sentence?"

"It's been on my mind, too. It's complicated for the both of us—you love Lee and I love Elle."

"We've gotten very close. I needed—"

"Someone to comfort you?"

"No. I needed *you* to comfort me." I paused, then forced myself to be really *really* real. "It felt good … being with you. I wasn't thinking about Lee. I was thinking about *you.*"

"We're friends, right?"

"Yes, we are. And you're very beautiful."

We laughed.

"What's happening between us?" I asked.

"Je ne sais pas, Taylor. But I am definitely attracted to you."

"I'm attracted to you too—which scares me. How can I love Lee and be attracted to you?"

"By loving Lee and being attracted to me."

"You know it's not that simple!" I protested.

"Alright, so I can see why you're a little anxious—you have a girlfriend. But haven't you ever looked at another woman while dating someone else?"

"Of course I have."

"So this is like that, only we're friends, and that's what complicates it."

"How do you feel?"

Sy said nothing.

"Sy?"

"Oui?"

"What are you thinking about?"

"I'm thinking about how I don't know what to say because if I say any more, I think I'm going to stop being a good friend."

"What are you not saying?"

"I like you. I've liked you for awhile. I don't like seeing you go through what you're going through."

"Sy ..."

"I'm not trying to confuse things for you. You asked me what I was thinking and that's what I'm thinking."

"I don't know what to say."

"You don't have to say anything. I just want you to know that I really care about you."

"Okay. I care about you too, Sy."

"Odaro, I know you do," Sy said tenderly. "But who's your heart with? Who's your soul with?"

"It's mad complicated ... but Lee."

"Then that simplifies things, non? "

"Well, yeah, but ... why are you so nonchalant?"

"What? You want me stressing like you?" she teased.

"I'm not stressed, I'm just ... *concerned*."

"I know how much you love Lee; that's why I'm not stressed. We both needed a different kind of comfort the other night and we loved each other enough to give it. Now I know what A.C. meant in her rhyme about crowded eyes. You know, you may not know it, but your eyes were crowded the other night."

"What?"

"Looking into your eyes, your eyes were crowded. I could see a little sliver of me, but it was mostly Lee. That's another part of why everything is so clear to me: your spirit is so intertwined with that woman, ma, can't nothing *nobody* do shake that, not even my fly ass."

I laughed. "I feel like I'm not allowed to be sensual like that with another woman. I feel guilty. If I knew Lee was laid up in bed with another woman, I would flip the fuck out."

"I know, I know. Je suis désolée. Maybe I should have—"

"Don't do that. I wasn't drunk. I knew what I was doing."

"So did I."

"It just bothers me because I'm not supposed to be opening up to you, my friend, like that."

"Are you gonna keep beating yourself up for this? Chérie, we didn't run off to Vegas and get married."

"It's not just what we did or didn't do, it's what I *wanted* to do. It's how I felt laying there with you. Of course there are other women that are attractive to me, but I've never acted on it, never laid in their arms all night. To me, being held can be much more important than sex because it's a form of intimacy on the level of making love." I stopped to think for a second. "This shows me how far apart Lee and I have really grown. I really miss her, Sy, and I feel lonely even when we're in the same fuckin room."

"I know it's hard, but what you're dealing with right now is not permanent."

"You don't know that."

"Yeah, I do. That first night I saw you perform, the two of

you—it's like you moved together, laughed at the same times, breathed together. It's like—you fit. That shit isn't everyday. You can't just walk out the door and run into someone like that any day you're in the mood for it. I like you ... " she paused. "And even I can admit that. Both of you probably just need some time apart so you can clear your head. How long has it been since—"

"Since everything fuckin changed? A little over three months."

"That's a long time to be going through this."

"Yeah, it is. I need a break from thinking and feeling so hard. Maybe I'll actually get some homework done tonight. I can't believe we have finals in a few weeks," I said.

"I haven't even *started* studying. I'm gonna get off the phone and go act like I'm in college for a reason," Sy said, and laughed.

"Ai'ight. Let me know if you need a study buddy."

"I will. À bientôt, chérie," Sy said.

"À bientôt, Madiko."

FOR SIZAKELE

atlantic & indigo

Dani drove down the busy thoroughfare of Atlantic Avenue in downtown Brooklyn with the ease and familiarity of someone who'd never left. "How long is your dance troupe gonna be in town?" I asked.

"Two more weeks. We came here to rest our minds and bodies before kicking off our tour in D.C. Moving back home to Detroit was definitely the right thing for me to do, but I still miss New York."

"I'm so glad you're here! I want us to do something fun without talking about my heartache."

"But that *is* fun for me—reminds me why I'm single."

"Ouu, that was below the belt."

"You're right, I'm sorry. You know I'm just playin though. Any time with you is good time. If I can help you sort through some stuff, then my time here is even more valuable. That's what sistas do."

We were a couple blocks from Sweeter and I remembered Sy told me she was working today. "I want you to meet a friend of mine! She's so ill, you two will love each other. She's working right now."

"Working where?"

"Sweeter—ou, take a right at this intersection. There's a spot right there." I pointed and she parked.

As we got out I asked, "You wanna eat while we're here?"

"I was *just* about to ask you if we could stay and eat," Dani said, looking over at me with a smile, the glitter in her lip gloss sparkling. She slammed the driver's side door behind her, dreads swaying slightly against her back as her stiletto boots clicked onto the pavement. She looked cute in her skin-tight jeans; she wore a studded leather jacket over a slinky sweater that clung to her and stopped where her booty and thighs met.

Stepping into Sweeter during the day was a completely different experience than at night. At night it was a dark haven, a soothing and soulful heaven, thumping Sade and D'Angelo, love and sorrow songs back to back. Although it was definitely a place to mellow out, during the day there was a fast-paced undercurrent coursing through everything, from the beat of the steps the waitresses took, to the rhythm of the rhyme that came to mind as I sat and watched the people around me. Today the coffee shop glimmered with sunlight that splashed in from the huge windows facing the sidewalk. A single lily stood in the center of each indigo marble table.

I saw Sy before she saw me; it looked like she had just finished bussing someone's table. Her tray was loaded down with dirty glasses and teeny plates with half-eaten desserts still on them. It amazed me how people could spend $5 on a piece of cake and then not finish it. Why not just rip the money up and throw it in the gutter?

"Sy!" I called from across the room. She must've recognized my voice because she turned her head toward me, smiling even before we made eye contact. Her smile vanished just as quickly as it appeared and was replaced by a look of shock. I thought she was looking behind me, but before I could turn around, I saw her drop her tray with a loud crash. She hadn't tripped or slipped; she just stopped walking and dropped it right out of her hands. At her feet lay broken dishes and shattered glasses, silverware scattered amidst spilt drinks and dirty napkins.

Dani and I rushed toward her until we were close enough to hear her ask, *"Elle?"*

"Syrus …" Dani said. "You—you okay?"

They know each other? But wait, why did Sy just call Dani, Elle—

Oh shit.

Danielle.

I stopped, and Dani continued to walk toward Sy. "Let me help you clean this up."

"You don't have to, I can do it." Sy knelt on the floor, grabbed the tray and began picking up jagged shards of glass. Her hands shook.

"Watch yourself, that's shar—" Before Dani even finished the sentence, I heard Sy exclaim, "Merde!" and I knew she had cut herself. Dani grabbed Sy's hand and covered it with hers.

"Where's your first aid kit?"

"I'll take care of it, I'll—"

"You'll *shhh* and let me clean you up. Show me where your first aid kit is."

Leaving the tray and the mess behind, they walked through a swinging red door that read "Employees Only."

I stood there with my mouth wide open.

Oh. *Shit*.

What. The. Fuck.

Even.

Just.

Happened?

shattered me with the memory

Vingt minutes jusqu'à ma pause. It'd been a busy day and Sy was looking forward to sitting on the curb outside Sweeter with a cup of iced coffee and just watching Brooklyn … be Brooklyn.

"Sy!" Sy recognized Taylor's voice and a smile splashed across her face.

Before Sy saw Taylor, she saw somebody else. She definitely saw somebody else. Sy didn't hear the crash, didn't even blink; she just stopped moving altogether. The loudest sounds she heard were in her mind. Elle screaming: *"No, no! You listen—fuck this. I will not be who you're trying to make me be. If you love me so much, why are you trying so hard to change me? Explain* that. *That's not love!"*

Sy's heart and head were clouded and crowded with memories. She was stunned—stuck within an instant that felt like an hour that felt like the two years it'd been since she'd seen Elle. It was a second that wasn't a second at all. Sy stared like she was starstruck, like she had lost all energy and will to move. Her hands were open, outstretched, as if she was still holding the tray.

Elle's voice
sounded like
the answer to a prayerful
wish,
felt like
an old
hand-knit
blanket.

Sy knelt at the edge of the mess, spilt tea and coffee forming a haphazard stream. Elle was talking, talking, talking, and Sy responded, saying things that she hoped made sense. Sy didn't know what she was saying, didn't know what she was hearing. A sharp pain shot through her hand, snapping her out of her haze.

"Merde!" She had cut herself.

Elle insisted on helping and Sy gave up resisting, leading her to the backroom, then into the more private adjoining office where the first aid kit was.

"Talk about a *dangerous* job," Elle said. When Sy didn't say anything, she added, "I'm trying to be funny here to ease the tension. Can you help me out?"

As the warm water in the small office sink ran over her cut, Sy let her eyelids be a curtain she hid her ache for Elle behind. Sy absently pulled her hand from the water and scratched her head.

"Sy! You can't rub an open cut on yourself, you might get it dirty and it could get infected."

"Sorry, sorry," Sy said in a low, distracted voice. Elle held Sy's hand under the water for another few seconds, then turned off the faucet and dabbed her hand dry, careful not to disturb the cuts on her two fingers. Elle reached into the first aid kit and grabbed some anti-infection cream, and delicately swabbed Sy's wounds with it. She carefully wrapped a bandage around each of the wounded fingers.

"There you go, ma. You've got to be more careful."

"Thank you—"

"Don't worry about it."

"Thank you, though. You didn't have to do all that."

"Yes, I did," Elle said softly. "I really did."

There was silence, but it wasn't uncomfortable. Elle and Sy had spent lots of time sans mots, just feeling each other's spirits. It had felt good to them; their love had taught them many ways to speak, including through and with silence.

"Are you gonna look at me?" Elle softly prodded.

Sy lifted her eyelids like they weighed 150 pounds each: very slowly. She looked into Elle's eyes for the first time in two years and felt naked before the familiarity there.

"So, uh, what brings you back to New York?"

"Dancing." She clarified: "I'm on tour with the acrobatic-hip hop-ballet troupe I told you I wanted to create. Remember?"

"Yeah, I do."

"I finally did it. I teach dance classes to young people impacted by sex trafficking and homelessness. We connect them with local organizations that can help get them off the streets."

"That sounds amazing." Sy smiled a real smile that warmed Elle's heart to see. "I know you must be happy."

"It is a blessing, definitely."

They were silent again.

"It's been such a long time, Elle. I was shocked to see you."

"Yeah, I could tell." Elle laughed.

"I guess it was pretty obvious," she said, embarrassed.

Elle reached to touch Sy's shoulder. "Don't be like that. I was kidding." Sy's eyes were tinged with pink from the tears sitting unsteadily on the lower rim. She blinked, and they ran down her face.

Elle tried to pull Sy to her, but Sy resisted. "Don't—you don't have to hold me just because I'm crying."

"I want to hold you because it's you, Syrus. Why won't you let me?"

"It's not that easy. I can't just fall into your arms ..."

"I miss you," Elle said softly.

"You didn't have to miss me. You didn't have to leave."

"I felt like I had to. I loved you *so hard.* But I had to go."

"How am I supposed to know that? You picked up and left everything we had without a word."

"I left you a letter—"

"A letter? You left me a *piece of paper* in place of your body. You left like what we had didn't mean shit to you."

"That's not fair, Sy—"

"Not fair? Really?" Sy laughed sarcastically. "What's not fair is you disappearing and not even letting me know you're alive. What's not fair is you never letting me close to you, even though I did everything I could to prove how much I loved you, to prove you could trust me. What's not fair is you randomly showing up like this after two years. Two years of silence, of nothing, of not a word from you. I can't—I don't even know how to love anyone *but you.*"

Elle leaned against the desk and sighed. "Okay, I left in a fucked up way. Maybe me showing up right now is fucked up, too. I'm sorry. None of this has been easy for me either, Syrus. I know you loved me, but half the time we were together I felt like you were really in love with the person you wanted me to become *for* you. That was a shitty feeling."

"Maybe you should have said that instead of leaving."

"I did."

"No you didn't, you just left. You can't rewrite what happened."

"I am not rewriting what happened. Syrus, are you seriously saying that you don't remember me telling you I was tired of you trying to change me?"

"I remember, but I wasn't trying to change you."

"Yes you were, you acted like you wanted me to apologize for organizing against sex trafficking."

"I never judged you for your work, *never.* I just wanted you to be *safe.* I was terrified you'd come home to me bloody and beaten by one of those men who didn't give a fuck about your job. I was terrified you wouldn't come home at *all.*" Sy's fear for and protectiveness of Elle flashed defiantly across her face, a testament to her love. "All this time, you didn't come back to me, didn't call me. I didn't move from our apartment for two years ... because I always wanted you to know how to find your way home. But you never came back."

"Syrus," Elle said gently, then whispered. *"Syrus ..."*

"Don't say my name like that."

"You know how I am; it's so much easier for me to dance than it is for me to talk. You're the only person I've ever let that close to me. I miss you."

"Every day you haunt me. The memory of you, the fights we had ..."

"I want to hold you," Elle said, stepping toward her.

"Why?" Sy asked.

"Why? Because ... Because I want to. Because my arms are hungry for you. Because I can't forget you. *Because.*"

Sy sunk into her like a pillow. Elle wrapped her arms around her, and a tiny bit of the anguish of their separation was released. To Elle, Sy still smelled so good. Not her perfume, just her skin, just *her.* Fuck ex etiquette and what was proper; they needed each other's arms.

Elle placed her palm on Sy's cheek; Sy jerked her head away and took a step back, the temporary peace broken. Elle sighed heavily.

"I'm sorry I hurt you," she said. "I wanted to introduce you to my family and take you back home to Detroit to show you where I'm from. That never even came into my mind as an *option* with any other woman I was with. I always kept my emotional distance with them. The fact that I didn't know how to do that with you scared the shit out of me."

Elle exhaled softly. "I couldn't control my feelings anymore. I felt my love for you—thick, pounding in my chest—growing uncontrollably. I cared so much about what you thought of me. I knew how much my work bothered you, so it started to bother me too. And then I was so fuckin pissed that I cared so much what you thought." Elle clasped her palms tightly together, as if remembering a prayer. "I hoped that if I left—left you—my feelings would go away ... They haven't."

"So you came back to New York to get back together with me? Or you just ran into me and figured, 'hey why not?'"

"Syrus, that's not—"

"Elle, you don't want me, maybe you miss me, but that's not the same as *wanting* me."

"You don't know what I want."

"Neither do you. The way you were holding me and looking

at me just now, it's more than an apology, it's *regret.* You left. I thought that's what you wanted."

"I didn't want to leave. I wanted to feel in control of my feelings again, and I thought leaving was the only way to do that."

"I don't understand you, Elle. Not even a little bit. It's like we spent all that time together just for me to really understand that I don't understand *shit* about you."

"That's not true."

"You said I made you feel shitty—really? Like, for real?" Sy felt betrayed by her memory. Was she remembering who she'd been to Elle differently than how she actually was? How could she have made Elle feel that way? "That's fuckin heartbreaking. If I knew that's how I made you feel, I would have done you a favor and left you."

"Syrus, I knew you loved me. I just thought you'd love me a little more if I changed," Elle said. "I wondered sometimes if I deserved you. Whatever issues I already had with my work were amplified by *your* issues with it. I was scared that you'd leave me for some wholesome kindergarten teacher or some shit." She laughed.

"Are you serious?"

Elle looked into her eyes and admitted, "Yeah, I am."

Shaking her head in disbelief, Sy uttered, *"Baby ..."* She rushed to put her hand to her lips as if to lock the endearment in her mouth. Sy's mouth was crowded with all the things she *could* say, lovingly, in that moment, but chose not to.

Elle's hands drifted to Sy's waist, landing tentatively like a nervous bird unsure of its footing and ready to take flight at any moment, at the sight of danger real or perceived. The familiarity of the rhythm and warmth of Elle's hands made Sy inhale deeply and close her eyes. Elle felt her own nipples harden as she pressed the softest of lips onto the side of Sy's neck and kissed her ... *there* ... there where she knew her lips always made Sy wet. Sy felt her body react to Elle, the embers of their passionate life together flickering inside her. Unexpected goose bumps raced over Sy's skin. The lingering resentment in Elle's heart was overpowered by her intense desire. They kissed a long kiss, full of memories, full of all the things they hadn't said and how many moments they'd missed of each other's lives. Elle caressed Sy's lower back beneath her shirt with a slow sultriness that made Sy's breath quicken. Sy lost her hands in Elle's locks, massaging her scalp while their breasts danced together to the beat of their deepened breathing.

thousands

I made my way to the counter and eased onto a stool. My movements felt too slow. Everything felt a little surreal.

Sy and Dani? Sy and *Elle.* Dani. Elle. *Danielle.* I never would have guessed. *Damn.*

It is a small fuckin lezzie world.

For real.

That rainy night in Dani's car, there had been a look on her face; a look of poignant regret when she spoke of her ex—Sy?—and the same look was on her face just moments ago. How could two people who were, and still are, so thoroughly wrapped up in each other *not* be together? They were obviously tortured by the memory of each other. I didn't want my relationship with Lee to be a result of what happened *to* us, didn't want an unintentional reunion or happenstance run-in to determine whether we ever spoke again. I didn't want us to have thousands of unspoken words caught in our throats years later.

Tati was behind the marble counter making a customer some macchiato something or other. Her normally tight curls were straightened, parted in the middle and layered slightly, giving her hair body. I waved at her; she served her current customer, then came over. Smiling, I said, "Hey, Tati. Your hair is cute."

"Hola, mami! Gracias, querida. You know I love me a good Dominican blowout," she said. She began drying a large pitcher with a dishrag.

"When Sy comes out, would you mind telling her I hope she's okay, but I had to go and I'll call her later?"

"Sure, no problem. Is that Sy's woman?"

"I don't know what's up with them."

"It looks *mad* intense."

"Yeah, seems like it. I gotta go. Later?"

I hopped off my stool and headed for the door, annoyed with Tati for calling Dani "Sy's woman." I didn't think I had the right to be annoyed. But I was.

So I'm attracted to my homegirl's ex? Whoa. Just … whoa.

I figured Sy and Dani would need some time to deal, to talk, and I wanted to give them the space to do that. Plus … I had someone I needed to see.

FOR SIZAKELE

the distance

the thousands of words
unsaid
between us
could line
the distance
from Pluto
to Venus
to Brooklyn

roundtrip

topography of our bodies

I'd headed to Lee's directly from Sweeter. Midday sunshine flooded Lee's apartment, filling her place with the warmth of spring. Lee was lounging in an armchair wearing basketball shorts and a well-worn T-shirt, the sleeves jaggedly cut off at the shoulders showing off hard muscle. Her feet were propped on top of the coffee table.

"I don't always have the strength to be leaned on," Lee said and sighed heavily, her chest rising and falling hard and jagged like steep, hilly terrain followed by unexpected flatland. "Sometimes I don't have the energy to be supportive about whatever activist crisis you're going through. You didn't even know when my fuckin game was!" she said. "It was a game that mattered to me, that I was nervous about."

She shook her head slightly and continued. "I don't expect you to come to all my games but I wanted you at that one. Taylor, there were flyers *all over* campus. How could you forget? All I do is practice—I leave home early *to* practice and come home late *from* practice. You're so out of touch with me, with my life." Lee met my eyes. "I want you to be my girl on the sidelines while I'm on the frontlines—for once. Just for once, can I have you cheering for *me?*"

"Yes, I can cheer for you," I said, defensive. I leaned against the window and crossed my arms.

"It doesn't feel like it. Before I met you, you would've never seen me at a poetry event, but I go *for you,* to cheer *you* on. Why can't you do that for me?"

"I do, I try … I'm not perfect, but I try," I said. "The night of your big game was a hectic night for me, Lee."

"Every night is a hectic night for you."

"This is the work I do! I'm a fuckin activist and I'm committed to it. It's not a part-time job."

Lee leaned forward in her chair. "I want to hear you speak about your commitment to *us* with the same passion you do 'the community.'"

"What the … Lee, you want me to apologize for being an activist?"

"No, baby, I would never do that." Lee's voice softened. "I'm not that selfish. I want you to admit you don't have time for me."

"Lee, don't, *please* don't …"

"Don't what? Don't tell the truth? You stopped showing up for me a long time ago. That's real talk."

I wanted to contradict her, but I couldn't. "You're right. I should have been at your game or at least made it up to you—and I'm sorry."

My apology seemed to melt some tension from Lee's face. "I appreciate your apology but so much time has passed …" she said. "It doesn't matter as much to me now as it would have if you'd said that months ago. These days, you won't even let me make love to you. What are we doing if I can't *touch*—"

"I hope this relationship is more than just fucking."

"Taylor, *please,* if you don't want me to eat your pussy, finger you or strap on you, that's *fine.* What really bothers me is that you won't talk to me about *why.* I hope this relationship is more than just being able to *say* we're girlfriends."

That hurt. I stuffed my hands into my jacket pockets. "How can you say that?"

"How can I *not* say that? Obviously you haven't forgiven me for holding you down—"

"How am I supposed to forgive you for that?"

"I don't know Taylor, I really don't know… and I can't say I blame you for still being angry. But what am I supposed to do? Apologize every day? I was fucked up, *I know,* but either we talk it out and figure out how to move on or we just quit each other."

"Is that an ultimatum?"

Lee half-laughed, exasperated. "Everything you *do* these days is a fuckin ultimatum. You punish me for my mistakes every single day. You're not the only one who's been through some shit in this relationship."

"You held me down, you accuse me of cheating every chance you get—"

"You slapped me. And threw shit at me, shit that actually *hit* me."

I was silent.

"Oh, I see. You don't wanna talk about that, right?"

"I'm sorry," I said quietly.

"You think because I don't beat you over the head with how humiliating, how hurtful that was, that it didn't affect me?" Lee asked.

"You don't talk about it."

"Why would I? Why would I let myself be vulnerable with you and tell you how I feel when you treat me like *this* when I try to open up to you? You shut down emotionally months ago. You won't talk to me. You won't open up to me. You're punishing me over and over. You fuck me like it's revenge. I don't even remember the last time you touched me … tenderly." Lee swallowed.

I was quiet again.

"I shouldn't have to ask my girlfriend to be soft with me," Lee said.

"Sometimes I don't want to be soft," I said.

"Taylor, you *never* want to be soft. Ever. Not anymore."

"That's not true."

"That *is* true, Tay, that is very true. You used to make love to me and *hold* me."

"I just don't feel good about letting you make love to me. I can't help that."

"Sometimes I don't feel good about letting you make love to me either," Lee said.

"Are you serious?"

"Yes. You're barely in the room when we fuck. It's hard."

"Why haven't you said anything?"

"Just because I don't say shit, doesn't mean I'm not feelin shit. I can't say I've forgiven you for slapping me but I know I don't throw it in your face every 10 minutes." Lee shook her head. "I know that you know you're the only woman I have ever let fuck me. I *know* you know how much trust it took for me to let you inside me."

"I do," I said. Hearing her words softened me like butter in the sun.

"We used to top each other and be bottoms for each other. Now, you always have to be in control of how we fuck and when we fuck. I wake up in the morning and you're *gone.*" Lee sounded baffled. "At first, I got it; I mean, I seriously fucked up, I should never have violated you like that. I knew it would take time before you'd want me on top of you again. I just … I miss fuckin you so much, I miss how you taste, how you smell …" Lee licked her lips, her breathing unsteady. "But I waited. I thought you'd let me touch you again—eventually. It's been three months and nothing's changed. It seems like you're a top now and I'm supposed to be your bottom."

"I never said …" I sighed. "I never asked you to be my bottom."

"Taylor!"

"What?"

"What is wrong with you? Why can't you just tell the truth right now instead of avoiding every chance to say what you feel?" Lee gritted her teeth; her jaw flexed in annoyance. She muttered to the ceiling, "Oh my fuckin—"

"I …" I sighed, slowly bit my lip and shook my head. My anger was exhausting, draining, sucking the joy out of every part of my life. All I had room for was more ways to be angry, more things to be angry about, more ways to push Lee away and keep myself safe from the possibility of being hurt, victimized, violated. Every moment of my days, these days, was sucked up and eaten by my rage. I was consumed with playing and re-playing every instance of Lee hurting me.

I settled into the armchair opposite Lee, the coffee table between us. "I don't ever want to let myself be in a place where … I could be hurt like that again, by you." I shrugged. "I don't trust you enough to let myself be vulnerable with you … so I don't let you fuck me anymore. I figure it's the easiest way to make sure it doesn't happen. I needed to feel in control of how we fucked so I topped you. It's like I was trying to make up for how out of control I felt when you had your hand around my neck." I reflected for a moment. "Like I developed an allergy to vulnerability. Sometimes, it's just easier to be hard."

"I want you to trust me again," Lee said.

"I didn't fuckin create this situation," I snapped.

Lee reacted as if I'd thrown ice water on her face. "Do you even want to be with me anymore?" she asked.

I was quiet. For awhile.

"Wow. Okay then."

"Lee." Our eyes caught and stuck. Lee got up and moved swiftly toward the door. "Lee, don't fuckin walk out."

"I just asked you—"

"I know."

"And you didn't say—"

"I *know*. But don't leave."

Lee turned back around to look at me. We hadn't spoken about this for months, and it'd been bothering me. "Why did you call me by your cousin's name? When you held me down. Why did you call me Chris?"

Lee's face crumbled.

I didn't look away. It would've been easier to.

"I—" Lee tore her gaze from mine and it spilled onto the floor.

"Look at me, *look* at me." Our eyes connected again. "Why did you call me Chris? Do I remind you of him?"

"Taylor …"

"What? You want to talk, right? This is what I want to talk about." My voice was hyper-speed. "Do I remind you of him?" I nervously waited for her reply.

"Yes."

I felt something collapse in my chest. Hope. My hope in our love—I felt it collapse and I felt tears coming.

"Taylor, *everything* reminds me of him. Spring reminds me of him, willow trees, my mother's face—because they look alike a little bit around the eyes; basketball because we used to play together before … The house I grew up in, my fuckin last name, *we have the same fuckin last name.*" Lee's nostrils flared. "I never go home for the damn holidays because I'd have to sit across a table and look at his face. Everything reminds me of him. You're the first person I could make love to and—and actually *make love to you* without images of him flashing in my brain. It's just sometimes …" She paused and struggled for words. "Sometimes no matter how much I love you and no matter how hard I try to stop those … memories ... of being raped by him under that willow tree in my uncle's backyard and afterward the blood *everywhere* … The blood everywhere … no matter how hard I try to shut those memories out, the shit comes back." She spun around and punched her fist into the door so hard she made a split in it.

I lowered my head into my hands and cried sad, angry tears. I had wanted—had tried—to love Lee hard enough to make it all go away, but my love would never erase that horror. That horror had the power to taint our love and I felt powerless, frustrated, exhausted.

I felt Lee sink onto the arm of the chair I sat in. "I ran into Sy a few weeks ago," she said.

"Really?" I looked over at her and saw her hand where her fist had connected with the door; it was beginning to turn pink, as if blushing.

"Yeah. She really pissed me the fuck off."

"What happened?"

"She thinks I'm a horrible girlfriend," she said. There was an edge to her voice. "Is that what you tell her?"

"No. She thinks you and I are beautiful together."

"Tay, *please.* That's not how she came at me."

"We're friends."

"Maybe that's the game she runnin on you—that you're friends. Meanwhile she whispers bullshit in your ear about me."

"Lee, come on."

"You come on. Real talk, you've been emotionally dating her since our anniversary. Don't front like all the intimacy between you two is just friendship. I kicked it with Ahsha *once* and you were wildin. Ahsha was trying to get at me and I wouldn't let her. Because of you. *You* though, begin a relationship with someone else under the guise of friendship and you want *me* to be easy? Fuck out of here with that shit."

"She's cute, I kissed her. That's it. I'm here with you."

"Are you too angry with me … to still love me? Is that what it is?"

"Just …" I sighed, my voice a little more than a whisper. "Just stay with me … and … I don't know. I can't reassure you, but I know I don't want you to leave."

After an extremely extended pause—a silence loaded with what felt like explosives—Lee asked, "Are you ever gonna forgive me?"

I sighed. "I don't know how to forgive you and I don't really want to."

"Do you still love me?"

"Yes."

steel

The next morning.

Early.

It was the kind where you can taste the dew in the crisp, spring air, like a barely there coating of sweat on a chilled glass of water. The awakening ruckus of Brooklyn's streets murmured in the distance.

"So what now?" Elle asked. She'd arrived at Sy's after their accidental meeting, at Sy's request. Elle strolled into the living room and draped her eggshell white scarf and black leather jacket over the back of a chair. She remembered that she'd bought the chairs and the matching dining table with Sy. Elle sat down at the dining table and looked around, noticing the sky blue living room curtains she and Sy had picked out; the aloe plant they'd grown. It still sat on the same windowsill, just as it had two years ago.

Sy was surprised. "You're asking me?"

"Yes."

"Since when do you ask me anything?"

"Since now."

"What do you want me to say?"

"Say whatever you need to say."

"Elle ..." Sy rolled her eyes, leaning against the wall.

"What?"

"Please." Sy sighed, annoyed.

"Please what?"

"Elle, what do you want from me? You want the rest of me? You came back to see how fucked up you left me?"

"That's not fair."

"You keep talking about fair! *Nothing* about us has been fair for the past two years. Nothing. There's a beautiful woman in my life that I can only halfway love because of you. Is that fair?"

"Who?"

Sy laughed a laugh that wasn't a laugh at all. "Why do you need to know who?"

"Can you just tell me?"

"Taylor."

"Tay—*what?* You love Taylor? Seriously?"

"Seriously."

Elle shook her head, then said, "You know she's my friend, right?"

"Well, yeah, I do *now.* So what?"

"So—that means something." Elle was flustered and defensive.

Sy folded her hands across her chest. "No, actually it doesn't. It's not my fault you disappeared. I'm supposed to choose who I love based on whether you'd be offended? Are you fuckin serious right now?"

"Maybe I don't have the right—"

"You don't have *any* rights when it comes to me. I'm only talking to you now so we can be done."

"Sy, what happened to you?"

"*You* happened to me," Sy said. She walked closer to Elle and looked down at her sitting at the table where they'd shared countless meals. "I spent two years pining for you and now that you're here, I'm angry—and done. You didn't even come back for me, you just *happened* to see me. After all these years, it's just a coincidence that we ran into each other. That's *sad.* So, yes, I'm done. Completely done."

"You can't mean that."

"What did you expect? Did you think because I was all shocked and frazzled in the café that I was gonna be a little puppy for you, tail wagging, pussy waiting for you?"

"Syrus—"

"Elle, *what?* Seriously, what the holy fuck do you want from me?"

Elle looked nervous. "I … want you to care about me."

"I care about you. Anything else you need?"

"I was scared. I left you because I was scared and I didn't want you to get to know me well enough to see my faults. I needed to be in control, and loving you made me lose control."

Sy collapsed into a chair and ran her palm over her face in exasperation. "After two years, that's the best you got? You have a fear of intimacy? You think I didn't know that already?"

"Soften up." Elle sounded defeated.

"No, you soften up! You *open* up. Otherwise, leave. You're good at it."

"You're not making this easy."

Sy stared at her blankly.

"I was really scared. I was really, really scared." Elle's hands trembled slightly as she twirled the tips of her locks around her fingers. "No one that I've loved ever loved me completely, not in the way I wanted. Women have loved my body or my independence or how I could make things happen, but not all of me; not the girl who's scared of heights and loves the trapeze and who sometimes feels ugly and who can't trust anyone but wants to."

"I don't get this. I saw all of you, as much as you let me, and I loved all of you."

"Just listen to me for a second—please?" Elle said. "I've been on my own since I was 15. I learned to never put too much stock in any one thing or person. So when I met you … I wanted to trust you but I just couldn't do it. A voice in my head was screaming at me to stop loving you, stop telling you my stories, to just stop. I learned to turn down the volume of that voice but one day that voice got louder and won. I listened and I left. I've missed you every day since."

Elle was silent for a moment. "I've been with other women. I touched them, closed my eyes and tried to melt into them, but I couldn't. Not the way I did with you. Your face stays in my heart and I compare everyone else to you."

"That's bullshit."

"It's true. Part of me hoped I'd see you while I was in New

York. I was way too nervous and scared to call you."

"You changed your number," Sy said.

"Yes. I didn't want you to call me because if I heard your voice, I knew I'd come back to you. I didn't call while I was in town because I didn't think you'd want to hear from me. But before I leave, I want to make sure you know that I really, really loved you. I'm sorry I left you in such a fucked up way. I'm sorry I left at all. You were incredible to me."

Sy sighed. "Elle, I don't know what you want—"

"I want you to forgive me."

"I don't forgive you," Sy said. "I don't. I told my mother about you! My Cameroonian mother. I listened to her disbelief and anger, listened to her 'wetin kind ting be this lesbienne ting you dey talk now?' I came out to my *mother* and she stopped speaking to me for a year. *A year.* I did that knowing that she might react that way because I loved you so much, so much that I needed ma mère bien-aimée to know about you—no matter the consequences. We were real to me. Not an experiment in how long a relationship can last before I bolt."

"That's not what you were!"

"That *is* what I was. That's how it felt. I deserved better than a note on a nightstand. We were more than that shit. Two years of silence. Two fuckin years. How fuckin dare you let me love you and then run?"

Elle sighed deeply. "I'm sorry. I'm really sorry. But you weren't perfect either."

"No, I wasn't. Does that make what you did okay?"

"No, of course not."

"Then who cares whether I'm perfect? Did I claim to be perfect?"

"No, no, you didn't, but I don't think you remember the ways you hurt me."

"Like what, Elle?"

"You tried to change me."

"How?"

"You wanted me to leave my job, Syrus, and that wasn't

fair."

"I wanted you to leave your job because I thought it would *kill* you one day, not because I wanted to make you over in my image!"

"My job, my life, my choice! Not yours. *Not yours.*"

"It was *our* life. Our *life.* I didn't want to lose you," Sy said, pained.

"My job wasn't right or good enough for you. I never felt good enough for you—"

"My goodness, Elle, how many times was I supposed to reassure that insecurity?"

"As many times as I needed. And then a few more. And then a few more. Because that's what love is."

"You wanna tell me what love is? Really? You're an expert now?"

"No. Clearly I fucked up. I know that. I fuckin own that shit. But you don't get the toll your nitpicking took on me."

"My nitpicking, Elle? What nitpicking?"

"Your constant 'why don't you get a different job, I don't know why you have to travel so much—'"

Sy shouted, "Tu m'as manqué! I missed you!"

"I missed you too! But I loved my job. I loved my work. It gave my life meaning! It made me feel *worth* something. I felt like I mattered. My whole life I felt like I was nothing, like no one would care either way if I was alive or dead. Finally I found something that made me feel like me being around was worth something. I needed that. I didn't have anything else."

"You had me."

"Yes, I did. But I had my work before I had you and I wanted to make sure I was independent. Like I wasn't solely relying on you to give my entire life meaning. So I had work. I was making friends for the first time in a long time, friends who liked me and thought I was smart. That meant something to me." Elle tried to hold back her tears. "So this thing, my work, which was huge to me—that you constantly wanted me to give up—was how I felt like I belonged on this planet and not in a ditch. You attacking that felt like an attack on *me.* It was exhausting. I needed to remember where I came from, I needed to help those girls get off the streets or at least teach them how to survive on them. *I had to.* No one did that for me but I wanted to do it for them, to be the kind of support I know I needed when I was one of them."

The air was alive with the words hanging between them. Sy bit her upper lip and looked over at Elle. "I didn't know that's what it meant to you," Sy said. "I tried very hard to keep you close because I could feel you fluttering farther and farther away so yes, I tried to change you to keep you, to make you stay. I didn't mean to disrespect your work or you. I just wanted you to stay, to be alive. I'm sorry." Sy was quiet for a moment, then: "You were always who I wanted. You were *beyond* good enough."

"Syrus—"

"Why do you keep saying my name like that?"

"Because I like how it feels in my mouth."

Sy swallowed.

Elle's eyes glowed the way they used to when they were in bed, with that late night, early morning tenderness. She got up and walked over to Sy.

"Stand up," Elle said. "Please?"

Sy stood. Elle put her hands on Sy's shoulders, then slid them down her chest. "Your nipples are hard," Elle said. Sy leaned in and kissed Elle. Hard.

Tongue hard. Breath heavy.

Sy circled Elle's waist with hands that felt like hot steel. She pulled Elle's body close and pressed her into the wall. Sy kissed her chin, her neck, her chest. Her hands hurried all over Elle's body with a hunger she'd bottled up for years.

"Sy ... *Ohhhh* ..." Sy massaged Elle's breasts, slow and hard, then slipped her right hand inside her jeans.

"Oh my God, Sy ..."

Sy's fingers drank her wetness, slipping over her hard clit as Elle shook and arched her back into Sy. Sy groaned deeply, guttural and uncontrolled. Her fingers sped up. Elle whimpered, eyes closed, biting her lower lip. "Sy, Sy ... Oh my... *Sy!*" She came shaking and pulsing, her heartbeat throbbing in her pussy. Sy breathed low, slow and heavy. She cradled Elle close to her, letting her body absorb the aftershock of Elle's post-orgasmic shivers.

Elle kissed Sy. Hard. But tender. Then pulled back and looked at her. They locked eyes as Sy licked Elle's wetness off her fingers. Elle kept her eyes on Sy's as she unbuckled Sy's belt, slid the zipper down and pulled down her pants and underwear. Elle descended to her knees, between Sy's legs, massaging the sides of Sy's hips with her fingers. Her eyes drifted closed as she kissed Sy's upper thighs with feather-light lips, teasing her, making Sy ache. She looked up at Sy until Sy's eyes met hers. Elle kept her eyes on Sy's as her lips traveled closer and closer to her pussy. Elle flickered her tongue over her clit; Sy tilted her head back, sharp and fast. Sy reached back and gripped the wall behind her as Elle buried her eager face in her pussy. Sy bit her tongue, then dug her hands into Elle's locks and moaned, deep and low.

Like a secret.

ঔ

Sy watched Elle walk out of the bathroom, fresh from a shower, eyes clear. Elle wore Sy's plush robe, looking like the countless other times she'd worn it. It was as if those two years hadn't happened.

But they had.

a heartbeat. a breath.

I sipped my too-hot hibiscus-ginger tea. To avoid talking.

Sank into the wooden chair in the café as I watched the people outside walking by. To avoid looking at Lee.

"Taylor." Lee said my name like a statement.

Fulton Street was alive with midday traffic. The beautiful people were out. Summer, or the close proximity of it, did this to Brooklyn—brought out the glistening shea butter-coated brown skin, the backless dresses, the open-toed shoes, the forearms and wrists full of bright, multicolored bangles.

"Taylor," Lee said again.

"Yes?"

"Do you want to be with me?"

"Can I order first—"

"Taylor?"

"What?"

"Are you ever going to forgive me?" Lee's question had an earnest curiosity that felt like hunger.

I sighed.

"What do you want—"

"I want to not have my every waking moment consumed by a few moments of hell," I snapped. "And I want to fuckin order some food. I'm hungry."

Lee picked up the menu and scanned it.

"I'm sorry, Lee."

"Are you?" She sounded skeptical; she turned the menu over and kept reading.

"Of course I am. I'm sorry I snapped like that."

"I don't think you've been sorry about anything since …" She raised her eyes to meet mine. "Winter."

"That's not fair. Or true."

"I think there's more pain between us than love. I think

you love someone else. And I don't think you have room for me in your life."

A heartbeat.

A breath.

"I love you," she said. "But my love isn't enough to love me *for* you."

"Lee—"

"I'm right." She set her menu down and waved away an approaching waiter. "I'm not angry. Part of me doesn't feel like I have the right to be angry. I came out my face, I lost it … I'm not asking you to confirm what I already know. I just … want us to look into each other's eyes, say what needs to be said and stop hiding from this decaying pain between us." Lee's gaze didn't flinch or budge.

"Something broke in us this winter and I shut down," I admitted to her—to her, and to myself. "Sy … I met Sy when I really needed someone I could come undone around, and not feel self-conscious or like my weaknesses would be used against me later."

Lee half-smiled in a pained way. "I'm used to losing precious things and precious people. Maybe that's why I'm so damn matter-of-fact right now."

I reached over and held her hand. "It doesn't have to be that way. You're not losing me."

"I already lost you, Tay," she said. "I've been thinking about my mother lately."

"Why?"

"I … I'm so angry at her. Still." Lee's voice was hard. "I don't expect any woman to ever be permanent in my life … and I think that's because of her. "

"I'm not your mother. And I'm not Chris."

"No. But we are still breaking up, regardless."

A heartbeat.

A breath.

"Right?"

FOR SIZAKELE

our mothers' recipes

"Syrus, it's Taylor. *Please open up?*"

I knocked on her door again. Unexpected nervousness fluttered inside me as I wondered for the first time if I'd done or said anything to make Sy angry with me. The thought of that possibility squeezed my heart.

No answer.

"Sy, I can hear your music playing, and your bike is sitting out front so I *know* you're here. Please, just let me know you're okay. I promise to leave if you want."

She opened the door. Surprised by the stricken yet guarded expression on her face, I searched her eyes for something familiar. Sy was enveloped in a bright orange and navy blue wrappa that crisscrossed her chest and tied at the back of her neck. Her feet were bare and her toes sparkled blood red.

"Hi," I said. "Where have you been? Are you okay? Did I do something to upset you? I've been calling you every day for a week ..." I couldn't help the barrage of questions; I was worried.

"I'm fine."

"Can I come in?"

She ignored my question, and started talking in the doorway as if we were already in the middle of a conversation.

"I was walking down Fulton Street on my way to work and saw you and Lee through the window of some restaurant. There were cups of hot things on the table. Steam was rising." She stopped. "Your hands ... you were holding hands. I saw you kiss her." She lowered her eyes. "Bearing witness to that picture of you two, I realized I've been in serious denial about our friendship for the past four months. Your love for her was *all over your face.*" Sy paused, then said, "It broke my heart."

"Sy?" I reached for her, but she turned away from me and

headed back into her apartment.

"You can come in." She threw those matter-of-fact words over her shoulder. I gently locked the door behind me. I'd never seen Sy like this, never heard her talk like this. Usually I was the one falling apart and she was holding me together with warm, sweet hands. Now here she was naked and unhinged. Her head was bent and her back was to me, hands on her hips. My heart beat wildly and I didn't know why.

"I'm not going to be the woman you run to for comfort to forget what an asshole your girlfriend is being." Her words were granite and tumbled rapidly to the floor. "I've been lying to myself for months, trying to pretend I can just be your friend, trying to pretend that every time I see you cry I don't want to hold you until you stop shaking. Every single time I saw something breaking in your eyes I wanted to scream. I don't want to be your fuckin *friend;* I want to cook you my mother's recipes—" She shook her head, resolute, back still to me. "I can't be your friend anymore."

"Lee and I broke up." I said.

"You *what?*" She turned around, her face a perplexed map of her pain.

"Lee and I broke up." I said slowly. "What you saw was us saying goodbye to each other. They are things between her and I ... that I am not ready to forgive. Our relationship stopped working a long time ago and I just didn't want to admit it, but at some point it started to hurt too much to ignore. I don't know what it was in me that kept me with her when it was so obviously dysfunctional. Tati has been telling me for a minute that I should be with you. I would laugh it off, ignoring my own feelings, feeling like if I admitted I was attracted to you, I would be betraying my commitment to Lee—"

"Walai! Abeg, I let you in to tell you that I don't want you to worry about me," Sy said. "But I don't want to talk to you about Lee anymore. I don't want to counsel you through your shit. I just can't." Her voice cracked. I stood in front of her and put my hand to her cheek.

"Sy." I said, insistent. "Chérie, ecoutes-moi: *je t'adore.* You're *amazing.* You mean so much to me—"

"Ne me parle pas comme ça."

"Why not?"

She pulled her head away from my hand. "Because you're holding back from me and I can feel it like a weight on my chest. I've been waiting for you to leave her for months, wondering how you could let her touch you when all she did was hurt you and dishonor you. I could never even think about hurting you."

"Sy, it's not like I was this helpless victim for our whole relationship. I was fucked up, too. I hit her."

"Exactly. Look who that relationship was turning you into." She shook her head.

"I know. I know and I had a hard time recognizing myself after awhile." I paused. "I like you, I'm attracted to you."

"You like how I make you *feel,*" she said, correcting me.

"Yes. You say that like it's a bad thing."

"It's not. But I think you like that I take care of you, more than you like *me.*"

"What does that mean?" I asked.

"I've been taking care of you; that's what I'm good at. Fixing things. Fixing people's lives."

"Why are you talking to me like this? Is that what all this has been? You getting to fix me like I'm a collection of broken bits you have to glue back together?"

"No," she said.

"Then why are you talking like this?"

"Talking like what?"

"Talking all cold and strange, like I'm a fuck up you volunteered to make better."

"Because," Sy said, "it's easier to fix people than to let them see who I actually am."

"Is this about Dani? Am I being lumped in with everyone who ever hurt you?"

"No. Yes."

"What?" I was *so* confused.

"Never mind."

"No, you have to tell me how you feel."

"Actually, I don't," she said, her voice hardening.

"Sy, this is what you've been doing since I met you. Something hard happens in my life and you offer to support me. I'm grateful. I try to ask you how you are—so I can be there for you, too—and you won't let me."

"Why should I let you support me?" she challenged.

"Because that's how friendships work. And now you're mad at me for not being there for you after you didn't *let* me be there for you?"

Sy sighed.

"Sy? Are you angry with me?"

"Yes."

"Why?"

"Because you let me take care of you. I think I resent that. I don't know how to let anyone do anything for me. It feels … foreign and wrong. I realize that's part of what Elle used to get mad at me about. I'd be sick and wouldn't stay in bed and let her cook for me. I couldn't stand to be weak. Or to need anyone."

"You and Dani—what happened?"

"Two years ago, or now?"

"Both."

"Two years ago, she left because she couldn't let me in. Me being protective of her caused a lot of fights. That, and she felt like I wanted her to change." Sy paused. "She's right; I did."

"Did you sleep with her?"

"We were together for a year and a half so … yes."

"No, I mean … recently."

"Oh. Yeah."

"You did?" I had not been expecting that response at all.

"Yeah."

"How the fuck could you make love to her?"

"What's that supposed to mean?"

"Didn't she break your heart?"

"Yes."

"And you can still touch her?" I asked, disbelieving.

"Yes."

"How?"

"Didn't Lee strangle you? You still fucked her afterward, right? Why are you judging me?"

"I'm not judging you. I'm …" I didn't want to admit it, but I was: "—jealous."

"Mon Dieu, de quoi? I've sat here and been your best friend as I watched you be in a relationship that I felt like an intrusion into."

"You never complained."

"What would complaining have gotten me? Were you going to leave Lee to be with me?"

"Did you want me to?" I asked, surprised.

"Of course I wanted you to."

"Why didn't you tell me?"

"Because I didn't think you were ready to hear it, didn't think it'd be fair to you. I was trying to be patient and a good friend."

"Was it … good?" I asked, knowing I shouldn't have.

"What?"

"Being with her, fucking her?"

"You're really asking me this? You don't want to know."

"Yes. Yes, I do."

"It was amazing," Sy said.

"You still love her?"

"Yeah."

I sighed hard; my anxious heartbeats accelerated their pounding. "Well, I love you." *I said it. I said it.*

"It's been, what, a week since you broke up with Lee?" Sy asked sarcastically.

How could she not be tender with me after I said that?

"No. It's been four months for me just like it has for you, Sy, and *I love you.* I want to cook *my* mother's recipes for *you,* I want to go dancing with you and laugh with you—"

"As a friend." Sy's qualification felt like an insult.

"If I was to be anything but friends with you right now, I would be setting us both up for broken hearts," I said. "I'm not ready for a relationship."

"Relationship? Is that what you want?"

"Yes. No. I don't know! I think so. I know I love you." Sy was silent. I continued, "Do you love me?"

"Yes. Yes, I do."

My heart flew out of my chest,
all over the room,
around the sun,
then settled back into my chest.
All in that moment.

"I'm tired of waiting," Sy said, her voice weary and resolute. "For you, for Elle, for everyone. I've spent so much of my life waiting, doing the right thing, and I'm fuckin tired of it."

"You and Dani get to talk?"

"Yeah, we did."

"How was it?"

"Hard. Really fuckin hard." Sy slid her hands across her face; her breathing was unsteady. "For the year and a half we were together, and the two years after, I thought she was the absolute love of my life and that there could never and *would* never be a woman I loved like that. Of course, that's still true; I'm never going to love another woman like I love her, because there is only one her."

She sat down on the couch and crossed her legs beneath her, then closed her eyes briefly. I sat down at the opposite edge of the couch, keeping my distance in case she wanted it that way. Sy continued. "I carried my memories of her around like … like a burden. She haunted me. I never let myself get too close to anyone, even friends, because I was convinced none of them could ever understand me like she did. I've been walking around with this self-created shell surrounding me. Women would flirt with me and I'd flirt back … but … I always kept my distance. I'd be attracted to women and I would avoid interacting with them so nothing would develop. Seeing her again … *completely* blew me away. Being with her, talking with her was like … a strange, familiar family reunion.

"She knows me, yes. But a lot of who she knows is who I was." Sy paused. "I don't want to be with her anymore. Our time together was so beautiful, so magical … but … it's not the same anymore. Elle and I talked, I mean really talked about who we were to each other, and she and I don't feel the same to me. I think I'm okay with that."

"You are? The way you spoke about her, she seemed like someone you still really loved and wanted to be with."

"I love her tremendously."

I kept my face expressionless as she said that, even though I felt like I was swallowing shards of glass.

"Elle, she's—I just really love that woman. The way I was loving her after she left—I was holding onto her because I loved her … and somehow holding onto her became why I didn't open up to anyone else. I would say to myself, *she's not Elle,* and I could justify not taking a risk and trusting someone with *me.* I got really used to doing that for two years. Until I met you. Despite all my efforts to hold back from you, I just *couldn't.* Something in me just couldn't, and after awhile I didn't really want to."

Sy openly looked into my eyes. No pretense, no subtext.

"You said you're attracted to me. Taylor, *I love you.* I don't know what I want to do about that. But I know that to be true. The fact that you're 'attracted' to me and maybe 'love me as a friend' is not enough. For me, it's not enough."

"Syrus Rêve Devereux. Madiko. Listen *well well.* Since I met you, I have been denying my feelings for you." I delicately peeled back my reticence. "I am much more than just attracted to you; that's just a safe way of saying it. When we kissed, I almost fainted; seriously. You move something so deep inside me. I've never loved an African woman before. You … make parts of me make sense that I didn't know another person could ever mirror or understand. I can be all of myself with you at once without having to define or explain who I am. You let me know I'm real. My African dykeness is real because I see myself in your reflection, I taste myself in your recipes, I hear my own rhythms in the music of your voice." My eyes were watery. *Damn, I love her.* "It's hard for me to say all this because I obviously have to stop denying my feelings, which even now I still am." I knew if I didn't tell her how I truly felt, she would pull away from me. "I don't believe in being in love, because that to me infers one can be *out* of love and what I feel for you is bigger than something I could fall out of one day. I love you with the part of me that doesn't think and consider, doesn't make rational choices or worry about possible heartache." I smiled. "I've loved you for months. When we'd hold each other and talk all night, I loved you then. I love *how you love me* and I love laughing with you. I already know this."

"Really?"

"Really. I don't need time to understand my feelings for you. I need time to sort through my relationship with Lee, because I don't want that unresolved pain to spill into this, onto you and whatever us we create … *if* we create an us, because … I want to create an us, a beautiful, amazing us. I don't want to hide from my pain in your arms. That's why I hesitate to say how I feel because I know once I say it, it will be so easy to just kiss you and pretend I ain't got shit to heal from and let go of with Lee. I know you don't want to hear about Lee; I'm not trying to use you as my therapist. *I promise.* I just want you to understand what I mean."

Sy was quiet. Too quiet.

In a small voice, I said, "It felt like you didn't want to let me into your apartment."

"I didn't. Because I didn't think I knew what to say. I don't have this—" she gestured back and forth between us "—figured out. And that is not my style. I like everything organized and clear. I don't like not knowing. So I didn't want to let you in, for us to talk and for me to say, 'je ne sais pas.'"

"What don't you know? What do you want to know?"

"Anything! Something! At least *one thing.*"

"Like …?"

Sy peered into me, her Fulani eyes intense and raw with emotion. "What I want. I love you. I'm very protective of you. I want to wake up with you every morning and go to sleep with you every night. I want to lay in bed with you. And hold you. And kiss you. And know that no other woman is touching you the way *I* touch you. I want that so much. I do." Her eyes were smoldering embers flickering, crackling into a full-blown fire. She was making me wet from across the couch.

"I've also spent the last three and a half years so completely wrapped up in Elle. She hurt me. Seeing her again was really good because I got to say what the fuck I needed to say. It was also a lot to deal with at once, especially when I had no warning that it was coming. So much has been going on inside me and I don't think I let myself be present to all of it at once until these last few days. It feels like I'm in the middle of an emotional whirlwind." She paused. "I kinda feel like we shouldn't see each other for awhile."

"What?"

"I … I need to think. I need to think really hard. I need to figure out what I want."

I was quiet. Then: "Can I give you a hu—" Before the words were out of my mouth we were across the couch and in each other arms, urgent warmth, hunger, love and sadness between us. I could feel her heart had let me in. She let me hold her soul, her worry, her love, her pain, her sweetness; I could feel all of her, I could feel what she'd been holding back for months, could feel her tenderness in the arms she delicately yet firmly wrapped around me.

"Why does this feel like goodbye?" I said. "Sy, I don't want to lose you." Saying those words made my heart and voice shake. She held me tighter. My tears swam down my cheeks and dove onto her shoulder. I clenched my eyelids, trying hard to shut out the possibility that this hug would be the last between us for awhile—ever?

"So after today, I just won't see you?"

I think she didn't answer because she didn't want to say the truth.

And so I knew.

FOR SIZAKELE

rose water

Summer Healing To-Do List

Week 1:

- secure summer job
- ~~break up with Lee~~
- get my CDs back from Lee

Week 2:

- let go of Lee
- go to Riis beach
- write poetry

Week 3:

- stop being attracted to Lee
- write more poetry
- relax

Week 4:

- deal with/dissolve my anger toward Lee
- call Sy???
- pray
- pray
- pray

The irony of it all really fuckin annoyed me—to find Sy: the rapture and laughter of her, the sweetness and humility of her, and then have to say *sorry I have to get over my last girlfriend before I can even be with you, peace.* It tore my insides up. Some days I was so pissed off, I could barely sit in my own skin. I wanted to rush my healing process to make my heart ready and I wanted her to know, without any doubt that she wanted to be with me. I tried to put myself on a timetable, tried to organize my healing like a rally or a meeting.

It didn't work.

My heart was stubborn, and my soul told me over and over that man-made time was no way to measure my heart's process and progress. So I stopped waiting, stopped counting days and expecting certain results. I started praying and dancing and writing and calling up my sisters to talk—and consistently got full nights of sleep for the first time in a long time. I talked to my plants, to myself, to my heart.

I *slowed the fuck down* and stopped thinking that it was up to me to save the world. I stopped attending every single organizational meeting on campus. I was actually shocked to discover that the organizations I was a part of didn't fall apart in my absence. I laughed out loud when I received this email from Xiomahra:

> T! I am so glad I haven't seen you lately! No offense. I'm just happy you're focusing on YOU. The last thing the movement needs is for one of our most vibrant, gifted leaders to burn out & self-destruct off the strength of overworking herself. Personally, when folks go thru breakups I don't think they should be expected to uphold any pre-existing obligations or responsibilities. That shit should be treated like mourning and people should bring you compliments, presents and ice cream. Speaking of which—what flavor you craving? I wanna stop by & check on you this week. Holla and let me know what's good, mami!
>
> kisses.
> xio.

I missed Sy in ways unexpected and sharp. I loved watching her in the kitchen. She was graceful and cooked like one improvisational afterthought after another—completely unplanned and perfect. Remembering that she called it "culinary freestylin" made me smile. I wanted to hear her voice like an afrobeat lullaby in my ear. I wanted to see every single picture she'd ever taken and hear the stories behind them.

Some days were harder than others. Some nights were torture. I'd trace fingers down my belly and into my panties ... whispering her name ... sometimes smiling, sometimes with tears tumbling onto cheeks and pillow.

More than any recipe or moment we shared, I missed Sy's friendship the most. For the first time since knowing her, I allowed myself to feel the depth and breadth of my love for her, and it shook me. There were times I ached with it and times my heart sang with it and I would laugh out loud in my solitude, *just from loving her.* My eyes traveled up and down our memories with care and honor.

I opened my eyes to the state of my life and realized there was shit I had been neglecting—like finding a meaningful, socially conscious, well-paying summer job (yes, it's possible). Like figuring out why I stayed with Lee when I was so fuckin unhappy. I figured I better get the hell out of New York for a little while and then I realized that running away would most likely have me running into what I wanted to escape ... so I chose to stay my ass in New York Fuckin City.

I looked at my ringing phone and saw Lee's name. Neither one of us had called the other since our breakup.

"Hello?"

"Hi," Lee said. She cleared her throat. "How's your summer going?"

"Fine. Yours?"

"Good. I'm, um, in therapy now," Lee said.

"What?"

"Yeah."

"Why'd you make that choice?"

"I ... realized there's a lot I need to sort through and I don't want to keep making the same mistakes."

"Wow." When did she become so self-reflective?

"It feels like an investment in my well-being."

Too bad you didn't make that investment when we were together and I could've reaped the benefits.

Rolling my eyes, I sighed and tried to be happy for her.

"That sounds like a really good thing," I said.

"Hold on one second," she called out to someone. "I'm on the phone."

"Who's that?" I asked.

"Ahsha," Lee said. "We're dating."

"Oh," I said. Ahsha had always represented one of those parasitic, bottom-feeding dykes who prey and lurk in the corners of relationships, waiting for an advantageous moment to rekindle a flame long put out.

And so I hated her.

My revolutionary, freedom-fighting ass wanted to kick her ass, sista or no sista, up and down Flatbush Avenue one good time just to *shut her smug ass up.* Did I say this to Lee? *Of course not.* But the fact that I felt that way let me know I still had some healing to do. Theoretically, when I could look at the two of them strolling hand in hand and not flinch, and not feel a single irritated thing, *then* I would know I was over Lee. Theoretically.

"Uh ... would you mind coming to therapy with me ... sometime?" Lee quickly added, "You don't have to if you think it'd be weird ..."

"You want me to come with you?"

"Yes."

"Why?"

"I want you to see me dealing with things head-on that I avoided for so long. I guess I just want to share my healing with you." I'd never heard her talk like this. "You don't have to come," she said. "We're having a bring-someone-who-matters-to-you night and I thought of you so—"

"I'll come. When is it?"

I was excited to see fellow Diaspora Soul members for the first time in a long time. Those of us spending the summer in New York would review last year's work and plan for the coming school year. Right before leaving my dorm room for our meeting, I got an email from Dani. Just seeing her name in my inbox made my heart jump. We hadn't spoken since Sweeter and shattered dishes.

Hey girl. This is a hard email for me to write. Can we talk?
—Dani

Ughhh. This is gonna be awwwkkwwwwaaaarddd.

I didn't want to be composing and editing my response in my head all night so…

—finger on delete button like trigger finger ready to erase vulnerability—

Dani~~elle~~,
Thank you for emailing me. ~~I know we need to talk but I didn't know how to reach out.~~ I'd definitely like to talk. ~~I feel nervous…is that weird?~~ When you available?

*T.

I hit send, grabbed my backpack and a light jacket and tumbled out my door. Halfway down the hallway, I slowed my steps and pulled my phone out of my back pocket. Hesitantly, I looked through my address book until I came to the Ds. When I found her name, my finger lingered over the number. I really, really didn't want to have that conversation because I didn't know what to say and didn't want her to be mad at me. I took a deep breath and called her anyway.

The phone rang.

And rang.

Relieved, I started rehearsing what I'd say on her voicemail.

"Hello?" Dani asked.

I sighed. *Why can't I just leave a voicemail?* "Oh. Hi, hi. It's Taylor."

"How are you?"

"I'm alright. You?" The hallway's green and brown speckled carpeting was suddenly fascinating.

"Fine."

"Dani, thanks for your email. I agree with you, I think we should talk."

"Well, it's bananas that you and Syrus ..." She stopped talking. "I never saw that coming. I don't know what to say. I'm pissed. I'm really pissed that you're with her. All the while knowing I really have no right to feel anything about anything. Which pisses me off even more."

"I'm not with her," I offered, hoping that would make her less pissed.

"Well, whatever."

"It's not *whatever,* Dani."

"Whatever you think you have between you two doesn't compare to what we had."

I was silent.

"Aren't you going to say anything?" she asked.

"I didn't call you to have you condescend my relationship with Sy. It doesn't really seem like you're interested in what I have to say."

"Of course I'm interested."

"It seems like you're mad at me and just want to snap on

me."

"That's not true," she said, defensive.

"Well, Dani, that's what it feels like and if that's the case then this conversation probably isn't gonna go anywhere. So maybe this isn't the time for us to talk."

"I'm fine to talk with you."

"Maybe you're fine to talk," I said, "But I'm not fine to be *spoken* to like this. You're the one who left. Two *years* ago. Now you're mad at me? I didn't do anything wrong. I met someone and I started to like her. Now I love her. Tell me what I did that was so horrible. You left Sy, came back and found out that she likes someone you know. How is *any* of that my fault?"

"She loves you," Dani whispered, like she was revealing a long-kept secret.

"She told you that?"

"Yes. You didn't know?"

"I knew. I just didn't know she'd told you that," I said.

"Are you going to be together now?"

"I'm getting off the phone."

"Wait," Dani insisted. "This would be easier if I didn't know you. If you were just a name without a face. But I *do* know you and I'm fuckin jealous. I don't want to be, but I am."

"Of what?"

"Of the way she talks about you," Dani said.

"Funny. For awhile I've been jealous of how she talks about *you*."

"Are you serious?" She seemed incredulous.

"Very. She loves you. A lot."

"I broke us. I broke her heart."

"But you didn't break her love for you." Saying that out loud hurt me a little. But I knew it was true. "You're coming at me defensive like I'm a threat. Or like I don't know that the love between you two was and *is* deep. I get that and I know that. I'm jealous of that and I can't change my jealousy or how much you mean to each other. I also love Sy. I don't know if we're gonna be together." *Scared to ask*. But I had to know. "Do you want her back?"

Dani laughed. "In a perfect world, my version of one anyway, we'd get back together. But … I don't think it's our time anymore. We feel more like a memory than the present moment—if that makes sense. I have to respect that. Also, I left her, and that's real. Her heart can't just stop evolving and beating because I bounced."

"So … are we okay?"

"You and me?" she asked.

"Yeah."

"If you and Syrus get together …" Her voice trailed off and I heard her sigh heavily. "I, uh, I don't know how to be your friend if that happens. I know I have no right to tell either of you what to do but, real talk, I can't watch that happen. I don't see me being your friend and watching the two of you love each other. I just don't. At least not right now."

"So we're not friends anymore?"

"No, no. I want to be friends; I just need time. I need time to think and really let go of Syrus. I don't want to lose you as a friend. I'm just being real. I don't wanna throw either of you shade or be bitter. I don't wanna be *that* ex—the one you run into at parties or restaurants and the tension is mad thick. That's pretty much what's guaranteed to happen if I try to be a supportive friend right now as if I'm not hurt and jealous."

"Maybe we can talk again after some time has passed …?" I suggested, unsure.

"Yes. Let's check in with each other after a few months. Sorry I came at you so hard at the beginning of our conversation," she said.

I felt sad, wistful. Like I was losing a friend. I didn't know if anything would ever be the same between us again.

"It's okay. I think I understand where you were coming from. I'll miss you." I said.

"I'll miss you too," Dani said, her voice solemn.

FOR SIZAKELE

tiger balm for the soul

Lee fidgeted.

Checked her watch.

Looked down the street in both directions.

Twice.

Lee had never been to group therapy—or any kind of therapy—until she started attending an LGBTQ Survivors of Sexual Assault support group. She arrived a little early at the LGBT Center in the West Village and waited outside for Taylor. It had been a week since she'd invited her.

She stuffed sweaty palms into the pockets of tan cargo shorts and shifted her weight from one white high-top sneaker to another. Her matching white Polo shirt was impeccable even though she was sweating slightly beneath it.

It was an indecisive July summer night—the air was drenched with a muggy heat and full of *almost ... almost ...* but not quite drizzle. The evening was not committing to rain, nor committing to the sweltering heat that simmered beneath the skin of the concrete. The weather lingered between thundering rain and an unfulfilled, pent-up energy. This is how Lee felt—in between and pent up.

Lee saw Taylor in a light yellow ankle-length dress and flip-flops walking down, then across, 13th Street toward her. The torso of her dress was a v-neck that fit her perfectly; the rest of the dress flowed behind her as she walked, an unintentional train. Clearly they'd both wanted to be early; therapy didn't start for another twenty minutes.

"Hey," Taylor said. She stood at arm's length, adjusting the strap of her dress unnecessarily. Lee's gaze locked onto Taylor's face and didn't let go. They hadn't seen each other since their breakup two months before.

"Hi. I know you didn't have to come, and it means a lot to me that you did."

"I want to be here. I feel a little nervous but something in me felt like I should be here," Taylor said. "It's weird seeing you."

"It's weird *not* seeing you every day." Lee's chest felt tight. She was surprised to find that she felt like crying. "I miss you, Taylor."

"I miss you, too."

"This is hard."

"I know." Taylor cleared her throat. "Can we go upstairs?"

They walked inside and up to the third floor, then entered the room where therapy was held. Lee sat down; Taylor grabbed a peanut butter cookie from the snack table and sat down next to her. Twenty wooden chairs were arranged in a loose circle. A few minutes later the therapist arrived and welcomed everyone. The energy and emotion in the room was palpable and vibrating. Eyes were wide open and hearts were splattered on sleeves.

Lee was the third to share.

"It's hard for me to be here, even though I've been coming here for a month. Every single Wednesday night I have to talk myself into showing up. I have to find new reasons, *better* reasons than whatever convinced me to come the week before." She paused, and summoned the courage to continue. "I asked Taylor, my girl—my ex-girlfriend—to come because tonight is Family & Close Friends Night. When I tried to think of who I wanted to invite, even though the thought of inviting *anyone* to hear me talk about my feelings is terrifying, Taylor—" Lee turned to look at her " —you're the only person I could think of. I want to tell you, in front of all these people ... that I'm sorry."

Lee got quiet and exhaled with a soft *whoosh.* "I spent ... eight years ... ignoring the fact that my cousin raped me and that my mother walked right out of the kitchen and didn't even respond when I told her. I have been *so* angry for so many years. I hurt you because it was the only way I could deal with my anger at that which I can never change: I am a sexual assault survivor, whether I like it or not.

"I love you. I know I really hurt you ... and that was horrible of me and I'm really, *really,* truly sorry."

Taylor's face was a river. She quivered, ever so slightly, in her chair. "A year and a half and you never talked like this." Taylor looked through her tears around the circle. "What did y'all do to her?" There were hushed laughs throughout the room. She turned her eyes back to Lee, her gaze as soft as dandelion seeds floating in the spring wind. "Lee ... my immediate response when you asked me to come was to say yes. Even before I knew what I was saying yes to. Because I love you. And you're my family.

"You really scared me. When your hand ... was around my throat—" Taylor breathed deep into her diaphragm. "I didn't know how far you'd go. And I think we lost something beautiful in that moment ... that we never got back."

Taylor shook her head a bit. "I know I shut down and tried to hurt you back. I *did* hurt you. I'm sorry I hit you. Shit is so complicated, I don't know how all this happened." Taylor paused for a moment, searching for the right words. "I want you to be free of the pain of what's happened to you, of what you've survived. It breaks my heart that you've been dealing with this for so long. I really wanted to love your pain away."

Lee's eyes were full of tears. "I know," she said. "I know you did. Your love healed me more than it may have seemed. *Please know that.* My pain never should have been your burden to bear. I love you for carrying my pain as yours for as long as you did. I know you really loved me."

"I still love you. You're family," Taylor said.

Tears fell down Taylor's cheeks. Glided down her chin. Bungee jumped onto her chest.

"You're my family, too, Tay."

ᘓ

"Thank you for coming. Really—thank *you,*" Lee said. They hugged each other.

They were outside again. The night was crisp and smelled of rain. The streets were a slick black. They stood facing each other in front of the building.

"I'm surprised you invited me and talked so openly about such personal things," Taylor said.

"Not exactly my style, right?" Lee half-smiled. "I'm trying to open up a little bit and talk about how I feel, especially when it's hard."

"That's beautiful. Thank you for letting me see these parts of you." Taylor put her arms through the sleeves of a jean jacket that only covered her breasts, and stuffed a matching clutch under her left armpit. "To be real with you, I'm still really fuckin pissed at you. I know I have to just let myself feel that for as long as I need to. Patience is a virtue, but it's not really *my* virtue so … yeah. But it still makes me feel good to know you're taking care of yourself. "

"I appreciate you being real with me. I know the hurt feelings between us won't just disappear overnight."

"They sure won't," Taylor said. "Patience. I know it'll also take time for you to forgive me for hurting you." Lee nodded in agreement. "Speaking of being real—you and Ahsha? *Seriously?*" Taylor shook her head.

"Yeah … I don't know what I was thinking. I'm gonna have to break up with her."

"Again?"

Their laughter felt like the tiger balm Lee's grandmother used to rub onto her body after strenuous, overzealous practices and games.

Healing.

FOR SIZAKELE

more rose water, more

Last night, after Lee's group therapy session, I had felt connected to everyone in the room even though I couldn't remember most of their names. In that room, I felt like I couldn't hide. At any given moment, my own sadness vibrated beneath my skin, so close to the surface that anyone talking about intensely painful things around me made me feel like ruptures of pain were exploding all over my body. I'd alternated between listening intently and tuning out completely. The eyes in that room were so wide, so shiny with tears, so fuckin real.

These days, my own tears come and go. My tears are exhibitionists one day—bold and loud. Then painfully shy the next—stuttering and hesitant. There was no consistency to my days, except the mourning of them. There were times when my heart felt like a block of dead weight stuck in the middle of my chest. Sometimes each breath was a labor. I'd wake up and for a moment I was blank—no pain, no heartache, just another morning … then like a flash my heart would break all over again in my remembering. Remembering the breakup. Remembering my pain. Remembering how much I missed Sy.

Every morning.

I took to ritual.

Every morning I'd kneel before my altar, spritz rose water on my face and pray. I prayed for patience with myself, with my sadness, with my anger.

When I had no words, I just knelt in silence. And breathed.

I lit candles in my solitude and prayed for the strength to feel what I had to feel to finally heal—not to heal so I could be with Sy, but to heal so I could be with *me.*

☙❧

One warm day in July on the phone with Tati, I smiled and said, "You're really trippin right now Tati!"

"T, I'm catchin feelings," Tati sounded confused and lost. "I don't know how to do this love shit. She's got me writing poetry—me, poetry. *What the fuck?*"

I laughed at her. "You mad, son? You mad?" She loved Montana so much and was so resistant to loving her, all at the same time, that even through my heartache, part of me thought that was … kinda cute. "Sweetie, I'm not the most optimistic when it comes to love, given my current state, but if she inspires you to write poetry, don't fight it. Let yourself be inspired."

"This is exactly why I never wanted to be with just one woman," Tati said. "Poetry, *me?*" I laughed at the incredulous tone of her voice, and somewhere in that laughter I realized I was laughing from a place I hadn't laughed from in a long time. A free, easy place in my heart unhampered by relentless aches; there was a sliver of sunlight creeping into me through the smallest of cracks. It struck me in that moment—I was *healing.* I wasn't *going to heal* at some distant point in the future; my healing was a journey, and my rage was just as necessary as my tears in my healing process.

Process.

I was in my healing process—my calm, enraged, confused, tired, unsure, depressed—my *everything* was my *healing.* I blew loving kisses all over my conversation with Tati and smiled as we got off the phone.

I danced.
there was no other place where I felt
as safe
or connected

FOR SIZAKELE

to Goddess
as I did
on the dance floor.
the more questions I had, the more pain I felt,
the more pain I felt, *the harder I danced.*
I put all my fury into my feet and stomped it out.
went to open mics and shouted it out.
would wake up in the morning and thank Goddess for my day,
for my breath,
for my life, even though it was a painful life at times.

I would go dancing alone.
to dance: *alone.*
not to hook up with a stranger,
not to impress anyone,
just to *dance.*
it was me, the music and the fuckin DJ.

I'd eat the music,
make love to the music,
layer my soul on top of the music.
undulations of my body,
sweat off my body was libation for Mami Watah.

movement beyond speech,

movement as the profound articulation of spirit
dancing:
the only place I could stop thinking and just *breathe*

dancing:
my prayer
without words

FOR SIZAKELE

what I

my blood
remembers
what I
cannot

FOR SIZAKELE

blood memories

The inside of my stomach quivered uncontrollably and I had no appetite. Performing naked in German (I don't speak German) for an audience of 5,000 in sub-zero temperatures would have been less frightening than seeing Sy for the first time in three months.

I went through at least ten different combinations of tops, bottoms and accessories, and not one outfit inspired me. Did I want to dress sporty-casual or sexy-come-home-with-me-luscious? I refused to cry, because as long as I didn't cry, I didn't have to admit how terrified I was.

The haphazard, multicolored piles of clothes on my bed and floor only testified to the futility of it all; the clothes I wore would make no difference. The tightness of my top would not change her heart if she was over me. My coconut-scented neck, mango-flavored lip gloss and aqua eye shadow wouldn't matter if there was no room for me in her life anymore. I might as well rock sweats, kicks and a hoodie.

No promises had been uttered between us. We hadn't spoken in several months, and I had no idea what I would see when I looked into her eyes—if she'd be livid or distant or even worse: pleasant but detached.

Sy had asked to meet up; she said she was ready to talk. It was late August. An entire summer had passed since our last conversation. *What if we'd waited too long?* What if it was too late and I could never hold her again? Never take the bus uptown together telling sweet, sacred, funny stories all the way up? Never eat mango in Prospect Park in the wintertime? What if she would never recite her favorite French poems from memory in the middle of everyday conversation?

I threw on a respectable outfit—loose-fitting orange-and-white striped linen pants and an orange tank top—and was out the door. Torturing myself with the possibilities was not helping; I might as well go find out what was what. The cowrie shells in my pocket comforted me.

We'd agreed to meet by the Piers. Both of us daughters of the water, it made sense. The Christopher Street Piers was one of my favorite spots in New York because no matter the time of day or night and—despite the persistent gentrification and over-policing of the area—it was always full of fabulous queers of color. All the children were out looking beautiful—in the midst of passionate voguing battles, talking shit, kissing face, holding hands, making memories, cherishing chosen family. Witnessing it all made me feel hopeful and alive. House music boomed through speakers somewhere further down the Pier. The sun was setting, blazing colors all over the beauty, the water and the people.

Clasped hands hanging over the railing, I bowed my head and prayed.

Goddess please ... I just want to be happy. Whatever your will is, I accept. Please bless me with the discernment to choose what's best for me, and give me wisdom and compassion for her and for myself. Please let me embody your love with grace and humility. Amen.

"Hi," Sy said, effortless as Sunday morning.

I gasped.

"I'm sorry! I didn't mean to startle you."

I looked out onto the colors of the setting sun sparkling on the water, suddenly shy, suddenly heartbroken. *Had she missed me?*

The water was so free, so big, so gentle and strong. I could smell the lavender of her drifting to me on the breeze. I remembered her sheets smelled the same way.

"Odaro?"

"Yes, Madiko?" I turned to look at her, gaze at her, letting my eyes kiss her. Her hair was picked out and beautiful, her eyes clear.

"I just wanted to say your name out loud."

My heart screamed unintelligible sounds and half words. My soul danced, but my tongue was still. If we could meet on a dance floor I wouldn't feel as awkward as I did, wouldn't be obsessing over how to express myself with the most eloquence. She had on skinny jeans and a white shirt tied behind her neck and again at the very base of her spine, leaving her entire back bare. She looked amazing. "Do you want to go dancing tonight?" I asked.

"I'd rather dance *now,*" she said.

Our fingers intertwined naturally. I followed her toward the music, until what was a distant boom-boom-boom synced up to my heartbeat.

At first we were passionate onlookers, and then we found ourselves in the center of a cipher of colored queers, feeling right at home with people whose first names we didn't know, didn't need to know, soul already knew. The bass was *bumping*—this was to be expected. I mean, we are African people. Everything made sense: African dance moves, an impromptu uprock, voguing for the fuck of it. We laughed. *Hard.*

We danced from memory, blood memory, and caught spirits, were spirits, kissed spiritually. We took it back and did the Kid 'n Play, dropped to the ground then wined back up. We twirled around each other, teased each other, were lusciously sensual, then hard like we got beef, then we laughed it off.

No words needed.

We melted back into the circle, becoming points that made up the circumference of this holy, sacred space and watched others enter the center of it. We raised our hands to the sky to give props for the flyest, most outrageous and unexpected of dance moves now rockin in the center.

Love in progress—*absolutely beautiful.*

Breathless, we tumbled away from the circle, fingers wrapped around each other like hammock strings. We walked the Pier, black sky all around. Still no words.

Water languidly ebbed and flowed around us.

"I dey love you," I said shyly. My gaze was glued to the ground as if an intricate poem was etched into it.

"You wan chop?"

"I could eat." I waited. "Did you hear what I said?"

"Wanna grab Thai? Barbecue?"

"Sy?"

"Seafood? Pizza?"

"Sy. *Seriously*—"

"Mon amour, bien sûr je t'aime aussi." Sy pulled our clasped, intertwined hands up to her face and kissed the back on my hand. "Now let's eat."

whenever I doubt myself,
I imagine a young Zulu South African dyke
who will discover my work in 2076.
I imagine her name will be Sizakele,
that she will feel alive and loved
because she will read her reflection
in these words.
she inspires me every day
to be the legacy she will need and want
to find in an elder.
I want to be here for her to find—in her past and my present—
when she comes looking.

for you, Sizakele

my.tongue.speak.
{outroduction}

A note on the title: Sizakele Sigasa and Salome Masooa were a couple; two South African lesbian activists who were raped and murdered in July 2007 in Soweto, South Africa. Sizakele was 34, Salome was 23; Salome's beautiful daughter became an orphan. They were killed for being lesbians. This book is humbly, lovingly named for them.

I started writing this story because I wanted to create what I did not see in libraries or bookstores: a story about Black dykes loving each other that wasn't erotica. Erotica is lovely when you're feeling erotic, but dykes are more than what is contained within an orgasm.

I wanted a warm, fuzzy, tender, loving story about the joys and pains of Black women loving each other. It started off as just that simple, but as time passed and I went through what I was going through in my life, I brought some of those experiences to this story to try to sort through them in my own head. More time passed and I really started realizing, *damn, what I'm doing isn't just me writing a cute, simple story; it's about speaking on the truth that exists between women, it's about us having a place where our realities are valued enough to be put down in an artistic, herstorical way.* Our lives, concerns and experiences are important and valuable enough to place in front of the eyes of the entire planet.

This story has always been about writing about our lives from our perspectives instead of being the subject of someone else's flawed perception. It's ridiculous that I have to even write this: we are dignified women with lives and concerns and we are human. I say this because most straight-identified, heterosexist, homophobic, heteronormative-supportive people don't believe this—although they will indignantly insist that they do. (A person does not have to be straight to represent on some oppressive heteronormative nonsense. Self-hate is real in these streets.)

The myriad ways dykes are dehumanized includes, but is not limited to, the sick fascination with: what kind of sex we have, how freaky we may be, what promiscuous whores we supposedly are, how we're most straight men's fantasy, how unnatural we supposedly are, whether or not we chose to be "that way," how we're hell-bound sinners and on and on and on and on and it *has* to stop.

We are not seen as human beings, but rather as a litany of problematic characteristics. We are not seen as mothers or students or activists or waitresses or dancers or mechanics or poets.

We are seen as just our pussies.

I refuse to allow that to be the dominant definition of who we are. We are people with issues like everyone else and we are people with issues *unlike* everyone else.

This story is about Black dykes. This story is about African dykes. This story is about immigrants and the children of immigrants. It's about who we are, but it's not just about love, it's about *how* we love each other and *why* we love each other in those ways. Sometimes the purest, sweetest love womanifests itself in such an unhealthy way that it feels like hate… and maybe it is. Maybe hate and love are so close—maybe we have to be careful of the ways we love. In a society that hates us, wants to kill us, erase us and re-pattern us after its own dysfunctions, it's no surprise that we have internalized some of those feelings and sometimes reflect them back to each other. We can't always love each other in the ways that feel natural, because in a lot of ways what feels natural *isn't* natural; it's what we've been indoctrinated to *believe* is natural. We have to learn to decipher between what's truly natural and the unhealthy patterns we have become accustomed to—like violence—that feel comfortable and "natural." We have to create truly healthy ways of loving ourselves and each other; otherwise we will systematically eliminate ourselves.

How do we create healthy ways of loving each other?

We have to make it up, dream it up, talk about what we want, pray about it, dance about it, write poems about it and never settle for mediocre when we know we deserve the sublime. Even if we're not sure we deserve the *sublime* because our self-esteem is fucked up, let's just *act like we know that shit* until our minds and hearts catch up and agree.

With all my heart: thank you for reading this, thank you for listening, thank you for bringing yourself to these pages willing to listen and read.

...bathe in the rose water...

Love, Passion, Laughter,

Yvonne Fly Onakeme Etaghene

aka I Am My Mother's Daughter

Jan. 3, 2001 - Atlanta, GA | May 30, 2015 - Oakland, CA
(Happy Birthday, Mom!)

Thanks & Praise

Thank *you*. So much. For bringing your heart, eyes, spirit, fingertips to these pages, words, heartbeats, moments.

I'd like to thank each and every member of my incredibly huge and deeply loving family. To my father, thank you for always pushing me to be my best; my brother Ediri, thank you for always being such a loving force in my life; to Jovi, Believe, Charles, Uncle Wilson, Auntie Dora, Auntie T.I., Auntie Okus, Auntie Omoni, Sister Tare, Sister Helen, Auntie Pat, Boyoboy, Grandma; all of you mean everything to me and I love you so much.

Aba Taylor, dear one, I love you so tremendously much. Thank you for your beautiful sisterhood and support. Thank you for listening to me, believing in me and taking care of me.

Aima the Dreamer, thank you for dreaming with me, for helping make my dreams come true, for your magic and generosity and brilliance. Diva Taurean power on full blast!

Aya de León, I have learned so, so, so much from you. For your open heart and endless wisdom, thank you.

Cat Burton, love, thank you for wrapping me in hugs and sweetness at all the moments I needed you the most. I love and treasure you so very much.

Chaney Turner, thank you for believing in my work and for being a part of making this book happen!

Dorothy Mak, thank you for your generosity and kindness and for all the love you poured into my work. I appreciate you so much.

Ejeris Dixon, sugar, I adore you. Thank you for being such a brilliant, sweet and loving part of my world.

Eunice Corbin, thank you for sharing your talent and for being a part of making my dream come true.

Jewelle Gomez, I carried your words in *Don't Explain* with

me to Nigeria to comfort and hold me. You made me feel at home at home. Thank you.

dream hampton, when I met you, you instantly offered to support my work. Without hesitation. Thank you for your big heart and generosity. And thank you for all the beautiful work you do in the world.

jessica Care moore, bearing witness to you being the beautiful, brave artist that you are inspires me to do what I was born to do. Thank you.

Lisa C. Moore and RedBone Press, thank you for being such a brilliant inspiration for Black LGBTQ literature. You inspire me so much. And thank you for believing in my words!

Margot Goldstein, your love is a gift. There were so many moments I entered into that I didn't know how I'd survive and you were there. I love you forever for that.

Martina Downey and Tawanna Sullivan, thank you for your support and for believing in my work. I treasure you both.

Megan Justus, thank you for your love, your gifts of lavender and tender friendship.

Natalie Delpelche, this book began on your birthday in Atlanta and after all these years, here we are! Thank you for your loving and constant support over the years and for reading draft after draft after draft. I love you.

Nic Bullitt, girl… you is magic, my darling sis, my let's-go-in homie. Thank you for your brilliance and wisdom and sisterhood.

Pia Cortez, love! Thank you for reminding me that my passions are holy and to pursue and fulfill them. I heart you.

Poetry for the People Crew, my poetic family, thank you for your exuberant love, heartfelt smiles and community. What I've learned from you and with you shows in every word I write.

Ryann Holmes, homie! I heart you and am so thankful for our friendship, our laughter and, of course, our mutual love of my mango cobbler.

Sugarcane Writers, our community has held me in so many ways. I am so grateful that I get to create art with you and co-create a LGBTQ of color writers' community with you. Thank you.

Sabrina Guice, dear one, thank you for believing in my work and for your magical fundraising and PR skills.

Selly Thiam, your work continues to inspire me. Thank you for creating powerful space for so many of us to tell our Queer African stories.

Simóne Banks, thank you for your amazing PR talents! I so appreciate you and your passion for my work.

Suheir Hammad, star, you shine so bright you inspire my own sparkle.

Contributors to my Indiegogo fundraiser, huge, immeasurable gratitude to all of you for believing in and supporting my dreams.

Zanele Muholi, you inspire me in a million ways and I am so grateful for your work, our sisterhood, your magic, your courage. I love you love you.

And again: *you. Thank you.*

Vernacular / Glossary

Dike/Dyke (also known as Astraea) was the Greek goddess of justice whose "companionate goddess" (some think they were lovers) was Aletheia, the goddess of truth. I love to use the word "dyke" because it is a jagged word; it disrupts conversation and refuses to be ignored. "Dike" was the name of a goddess that was turned into a slur, whereas some of the words that LGBTQ folks, Black people and people of color identify with are slurs that were reclaimed, flipped and transformed into something positive. There is no need to flip the paradigm with this word; all we need to do is return to its beautiful origin.

Pillow Princess: The term "pillow princess" refers to a woman, typically a femme woman, who never gives pleasure, only receives it. The stereotype is one where she is always on her back in bed, lying on a pillow being pleased hence the term "pillow princess." This term is often used as an insult and infers that said pillow princess is a selfish lover.

Trigger: to remind someone of something painful; to become lost in a traumatic memory; an event or moment that acts as catalyst to aforementioned, therefore causing one to relive the trauma and the traumatic emotions therein.

Beautiful Reading
{lovingly compiled}

When I started writing *For Sizakele*, I was 20 and hungry for stories in which I could see my own reflection. I wanted to read stories about women loving and fucking each other. If you're looking for verses and stories that will feel like home to you, dive into this list. This is in no way meant to be a list of every queer colored story and poem ever written; it's a list of some of the writing that has moved me and continues to move me. Not all these books are queer, but the vast majority of them are.

Poetry, Fiction and Multi-Genre Writing

Achebe, Chinua. *Things Fall Apart*

Baldwin, James. *Another Country* and *The Fire Next Time*

Bridgforth, Sharon. *love/conjure blues; the bull-jean stories;* and *delta dandi*

Butler, Octavia. *Fledgling* and *Bloodchild and Other Stories*

Chrystos. *In Her I Am*

Etaghene, Yvonne Fly Onakeme. *Afrocrown: Fierce Poetry; write or die; tongue twisted transcontinental sista;* and *skin into verse*

Gomez, Jewelle. *Don't Explain* and *The Gilda Stories*

Hardy, James Earl. *B-Boy Blues*

Ford, T'ai Freedom. www.shesaidword.com/

Hammad, Suheir. *ZaatarDiva*

Hansberry, Lorraine. *To Be Young, Gifted and Black*

Hopkinson, Nalo. *Brown Girl in the Ring*

Jordan, June. *Directed by Desire: The Collected Poems of June Jordan* and *Some of Us Did Not Die: New and Selected Essays*

Kincaid, Jamaica. *A Small Place*

Lorde, Audre. *I Am Your Sister: Collected and Unpublished Writings of Audre Lorde,* ed. by Rudolph Byrd, Johnetta B. Cole and Beverly Guy-Sheftall; and *Sister Outsider: Essays and Speeches*

Moïse, Lenelle. Everything she does and says! www.lenellemoise.com

Mosley, Walter. *This Year You Write Your Novel*

Parker, Pat. *Movement in Black*

Shange, Ntozake. *for colored girls who have considered suicide/ when the rainbow is enuf*

Shire, Warsan. *Teaching My Mother How to Give Birth*

Smith, Barbara. *The Truth That Never Hurts: Writings on Race, Gender and Freedom;* and "Toward a Black Feminist Criticism," in *All the Women Are White, All the Blacks Are Men, But Some of Us Are Brave: Black Women's Studies,* ed. by Gloria T. Hull, Patricia Bell Scott and Barbara Smith

Sneed, Pamela. *Imagine Being More Afraid of Freedom Than Slavery*

Waheed, Nayyirah. *salt.*

Youngblood, Shay. *Soul Kiss*

Anthologies

Moore, Lisa C. ed. *does your mama know? An Anthology of Black Lesbian Coming Out Stories*

Silvera, Makeda, ed. *Piece of My Heart: A Lesbian of Colour Anthology*

Smartt, Dorothea and Bernadette Halpin, eds. *Words from the Women's Cafe*

Photography

Muholi, Zanele. *Only Half the Picture* and *Faces and Phases*

Film

Bocahut, Laurent and Philip Brooks. *Woubi Chéri*

Hewitt, C. Sala. *Good Lookin' Out*

McClodden, Tiona. *black./womyn.: conversations*

Rees, Dee. *Pariah*

Taylor, Aba. *Coming in America*

Ude, Ije. *The Visit*

Walidah, Hanifah. *Black Folks Guide to Black Folks* (a performance piece) and *U People* (film)

Williams, Karen. *I Need a Snack*

Mamabolo, Makgano and Lodi Matsetela. *Society* (South African television drama series) www.tvsa.co.za/shows/viewshowabout.aspx?showid=119

Blogs and Websites

bklyn boihood. www.bklynboihood.com

Cortez, Pia. www.piathabia.com

Etaghene, Yvonne Fly Onakeme. "hard. femme. prayer." youtu.be/FYK1wwvXs78

Gumbs, Alexis Pauline. brokenbeautiful.wordpress.com/

Johnson, Cyree Jarelle. "Femme Privilege Does Not Exist" femmedreamboat.tumblr.com/post/39734380982/femme-privilege-does-not-exist

Minott, Zinzi. "The Reluctant Femme. Femme"
http://elixher.com/the-reluctant-femme-femme/

Muholi, Zanele. www.stevenson.info/artists/muholi.html

None on Record. www.youtube.com/NoneOnRecord

Who I Be

Oakland Based. New York Gully. Nigerian Soul. **Yvonne Fly Onakeme Etaghene** is an Ijaw and Urhobo Nigerian dyke performance activist, poet, dancer, educator, actress and mixed-media visual artist who was born with a mouth full of dynamite and sugarcane. Etaghene engages a radical vulnerability and candor in her art and uses storytelling to build authentic human connection through passionate artistic expression.

Etaghene has rocked stages and melted microphones internationally, and toured with her one-woman shows, *Volcano's Birthright{s}* and *GUAVA*. In May 2012, Etaghene founded Sugarcane, an LGBTQ of color writing workshop series based in the principles of June Jordan's Poetry for the People. She designed an eight-week curriculum and syllabus for Sugarcane that centers LGBTQ of color, immigrant and immigrant-descendant literary and performative voices.

Etaghene has produced four solo visual art exhibitions and directed two poem videos, "The First Time" (2010) and "i deserve somebody" (2011), that marry film, poetry and music. Etaghene published four chapbooks of poetry: *afrocrown: fierce poetry* (2000), *write or die* (2004), *tongue twisted transcontinental sista* (2006), and *skin into verse* (2014). She released an album of poetry and music titled *liberty avenue, nigeria, usa* (2004.) She was interviewed by and was a contributing writer to None on Record: Stories of Queer Africa, a digital media project that collects stories of LGBTI Africans from the African continent and the diaspora. In 2014, she was one of *Go Magazine*'s 100 Women We Love.

Her second album of poetry, *Nigerian Dyke Realness,* drops in 2015.

For Sizakele is Etaghene's first novel.

www.myloveisaverb.com
www.twitter.com/myloveisaverb
www.youtube.com/AfrocrownDiva
www.facebook.com/trustyourpassion